THE HEART'S PRIZE

Elmina put her head a little to one side as she asked her new husband: "What do you enjoy most in your life? What gives you the greatest pleasure?"

The Marquis thought an appropriate reply to the question could be, "Making love," but he felt in the circumstances it would be somewhat embarrassing. Therefore, thinking quickly, he replied: "It is difficult to answer, but perhaps winning a race in a close finish."

"Exactly!" Elmina cried. "And it is the same with hunting. To every sportsman, the real enjoyment is the excitement of the race."

The Marquis was silent after she had finished speaking. Then unexpectedly he laughed.

"Are you really saying to me that I have to chase you as if you were a fox, or win a race in which you are the prize, before you will consent to be my wife in anything but name?"

There was a pause before Elmina, with a faint flush on her cheeks, nodded.

A VERY UNUSUAL WIFE

A Camfield Novel of Love

Camfield Place,
Hatfield
Hertfordshire,
England

Dearest Reader,

Camfield Novels of Love mark a very exciting era of my books with Jove. They already have nearly two hundred of my books which they have had ever since they became my first publisher in America. Now all my original paperback romances in the future will be published by them.

As you already know, Camfield Place in Hertfordshire is my home, which originally existed in 1275, but was rebuilt in 1867 by the grandfather of Beatrix Potter.

It was here in this lovely house, with the best view of the county, that she wrote *The Tale of Peter Rabbit*. Mr. McGregor's garden is exactly as she described it. The door in the wall that the fat little rabbit could not squeeze underneath and the goldfish pool where the white cat sat twitching its tail are still there.

I had Camfield Place blessed when I came here in 1950 and was so happy with my husband until he died, and now with my children and grandchildren, that I know the atmosphere is filled with love and we have all been very lucky.

It is easy here to write of love and I know you will enjoy the Camfield Novels of Love. Their plots are definitely exciting and the covers very romantic. They come to you, like all my books, with love.

Bless you,

Books by Barbara Cartland

THE ADVENTURER
AGAIN THIS RAPTURE
ARMOUR AGAINST
  LOVE
THE AUDACIOUS
  ADVENTURESS
BARBARA CARTLAND'S
  BOOK OF BEAUTY
  AND HEALTH
THE BITTER WINDS OF
  LOVE
BLUE HEATHER
BROKEN BARRIERS
THE CAPTIVE HEART
THE COIN OF LOVE
THE COMPLACENT WIFE
COUNT THE STARS
CUPID RIDES PILLION
DANCE ON MY HEART
DESIRE OF THE HEART
DESPERATE DEFIANCE
THE DREAM WITHIN
A DUEL OF HEARTS
ELIZABETH EMPRESS OF
  AUSTRIA
ELIZABETHAN LOVER
THE ENCHANTED
  MOMENT
THE ENCHANTED
  WALTZ
THE ENCHANTING EVIL
ESCAPE FROM PASSION
FOR ALL ETERNITY
A GHOST IN MONTE
  CARLO
THE GOLDEN GONDOLA
A HALO FOR THE DEVIL
A HAZARD OF HEARTS
A HEART IS BROKEN
THE HEART OF THE
  CLAN
THE HIDDEN EVIL
THE HIDDEN HEART
THE HORIZONS OF LOVE
AN INNOCENT IN
  MAYFAIR
IN THE ARMS OF LOVE
THE IRRESISTIBLE BUCK

JOSEPHINE EMPRESS OF
  FRANCE
THE KISS OF PARIS
THE KISS OF THE DEVIL
A KISS OF SILK
THE KNAVE OF HEARTS
THE LEAPING FLAME
A LIGHT TO THE HEART
LIGHTS OF LOVE
THE LITTLE PRETENDER
LOST ENCHANTMENT
LOST LOVE
LOVE AND LINDA
LOVE AT FORTY
LOVE FORBIDDEN
LOVE HOLDS THE
  CARDS
LOVE IN HIDING
LOVE IN PITY
LOVE IS AN EAGLE
LOVE IS CONTRABAND
LOVE IS DANGEROUS
LOVE IS MINE
LOVE IS THE ENEMY
LOVE ME FOREVER
LOVE ON THE RUN
LOVE TO THE RESCUE
LOVE UNDER FIRE
THE MAGIC OF HONEY
MESSENGER OF LOVE
METTERNICH: THE
  PASSIONATE
  DIPLOMAT
MONEY, MAGIC AND
  MARRIAGE
NO HEART IS FREE
THE ODIOUS DUKE
OPEN WINGS
OUT OF REACH
THE PASSIONATE
  PILGRIM
THE PRETTY
  HORSEBREAKERS
THE PRICE IS LOVE
A RAINBOW TO HEAVEN
THE RELUCTANT BRIDE
THE SCANDALOUS LIFE
  OF KING CAROL

THE SECRET FEAR
THE SMUGGLED HEART
A SONG OF LOVE
STARS IN MY HEART
STOLEN HALO
SWEET ADVENTURE
SWEET ENCHANTRESS
SWEET PUNISHMENT
THEFT OF A HEART
THE THIEF OF LOVE
THIS TIME IT'S LOVE
TOUCH A STAR
TOWARDS THE STARS
THE UNKNOWN HEART
THE UNPREDICTABLE
  BRIDE
A VIRGIN IN PARIS
WE DANCED ALL NIGHT
WHERE IS LOVE?
THE WINGS OF ECSTASY
THE WINGS OF LOVE
WINGS ON MY HEART
WOMAN, THE ENIGMA

CAMFIELD
NOVELS OF LOVE

THE POOR GOVERNESS
WINGED VICTORY
LUCKY IN LOVE
LOVE AND THE MARQUIS
A MIRACLE IN MUSIC
LIGHT OF THE GODS
BRIDE TO A BRIGAND
LOVE COMES WEST
A WITCH'S SPELL
SECRETS
THE STORMS OF LOVE
MOONLIGHT ON THE
  SPHINX
WHITE LILAC
REVENGE OF THE HEART
THE ISLAND OF LOVE
THERESA AND A TIGER
LOVE IS HEAVEN
MIRACLE FOR A
  MADONNA
A VERY UNUSUAL WIFE

A NEW CAMFIELD NOVEL OF LOVE BY

BARBARA CARTLAND

A Very Unusual Wife

A JOVE BOOK

A VERY UNUSUAL WIFE

A Jove Book/published by arrangement with
the author

PRINTING HISTORY
Jove edition/March 1985

ISBN: 0-515-08040-3

Jove books are published by The Berkley Publishing Group,
200 Madison Avenue, New York, N.Y. 10016.
The words "A JOVE BOOK" and the "J" with sunburst
are trademarks belonging to Jove Publications, Inc.

PRINTED IN THE UNITED STATES OF AMERICA

Author's Note

THE basic psychological principles of *Karate* are concentration, calmness and confidence.

Bare-handed fighting was being developed in both India and China before Bodhidharma first arrived in China in A.D. 520. He was, however, called the "original propagator of the Martial Arts concept."

With a special breathing technique, he created the basis for the legendary system of weaponless fighting and mental concentration.

Kung Fu was Buddhist-inspired, and for centuries Buddhist monks in China and Japan have studied *Kempo*.

Ju Jitsu differs in that blows are struck not with the clenched fist but with the minor or little-finger edge of the palm.

Ju Jitsu does not depend as much on the psychological side of the Art as *Karate*.

On the monument of its most famous teacher, Funakoshi, is written: "There are no offensive techniques in *Karate*."

chapter one

1846

The Earl of Warnborough threw the letters he had opened down on the table with what sounded suspiciously like an oath.

"Bills! Bills! Bills!" he said. "Do I ever get anything else in this house? I cannot imagine how you can spend so much money!"

He looked across the table in a hostile manner at his wife who merely replied:

"I am sorry, George dear, but things are very expensive at the moment, and I do try to economise!"

"Then all I can say is that you are not very successful," the Earl said disagreeably, "and it means I shall have to give up the hounds!"

There was a cry at this from all his three daughters, who were sitting round the table.

"Oh, no, Papa! You cannot do that!"

"I shall have to," the Earl said gloomily. "What with the horses eating their heads off, wages rising, and you girls becoming more expensive every day, things cannot go on as they are."

"You have been very generous to me, Papa," Lady Mirabel, his eldest daughter said, "and although I know you grudge the money Mama had to pay for my gowns, Robert Warrington has proposed and as soon as he is out of mourning, we shall be married."

There was a faint smile on the Earl's lips as he remembered how rich his future son-in-law was.

He had rather hoped that since Mirabel was so lovely she would marry a man with a more important title.

But Sir Robert was the Seventh Baronet and, what was even more pleasing, he was extremely wealthy.

He had fallen in love with Mirabel and would have married her at the end of last year if he had not been in mourning for his mother, who had been in ailing health for some years.

He was, however, determined that they should be married in November, and Mirabel was now thinking apprehensively that it would be disastrous if her father refused to pay for the elaborate and expensive trousseau she and her mother were planning.

As if the Countess were thinking the same thing she said coaxingly: "I am sure, George dear, as you are so clever, you will find some way out of our difficulties, and I know it would break the girls' hearts if you really gave up the hounds."

She was thinking it would also break her husband's heart, for he adored the pack of which he had been

Master for over fifteen years, taking over from his father before him.

It was so much a part of their existence that it was impossible for those sitting round the breakfast-table to imagine Warne Park without the Meets which took place there every season.

There was also the Hunt Ball when the Ball-Room was filled with pink-coated men and elegantly gowned women, and the Hunt Breakfast at which the Earl was specially hospitable to any new members, as well as to those who had supported the Hunt for years.

"We have to economise somewhere," he said in a firm voice, "and if you are suggesting that I should sell anything in the house, the answer is 'No!' Everything has to be kept for Desmond, which is only fair."

The way he spoke made his daughters glance at each other with a knowing look in their eyes and a smile on their lips.

They all knew that Desmond was the 'apple of his father's eye.' They had only to suggest that in a few years he would want the hounds to remain as they were, and the economies would have to come from somewhere else.

After fathering three daughters and finding the third was a dismal disappointment when he had so eagerly wanted a son, the Earl had given up hope of having an heir.

Then, almost like a miracle, when his wife had thought that a fourth child was impossible, Desmond had arrived.

He was the son the Earl had always wanted and he was in fact, completely besotted by the small boy, now four, who was still in the Nursery, but for whom great plans had been made for the future.

First the best Public School, the best University, and what could be better than Eton and Oxford?

Then of course, after a trip round the world to 'widen his horizons' as the Earl said grandly, he would help his father look after the Estate until it became his.

Almost as if they had rehearsed it together, Mirabel and Deirdre now said as one voice:

"But you must be aware, Papa, that Desmond will want to ride with our own hounds and of course become Master of them when you are too old to carry on."

On the other side of the table Lady Elmina's eyes were twinkling as she knew that without having to fight a battle that meant even more to her than to either of her sisters, victory was assured.

Not that she was really apprehensive, knowing how much her father loved his horses and looked forward all the year to when the Hunting season came round again.

She had the feeling that however much he groaned and grumbled he would be prepared to sell the clothes off his daughters' backs rather than part with something which meant so much to him and, as it happened, to her.

The Earl, having been bitterly disappointed that his third child was yet another girl, had treated her in a different way from his two elder daughters.

It was strangely enough with Elmina that he discussed the running of the Estate and the well-being of his horses.

She helped him with the training of the young animals he bred or bought cheap and turned them into first-class hunters for himself and his family, or else sold them at a good profit.

It was Elmina who went out shooting with him in the Autumn if he had no other guests, and trudged over the fields in the wind and rain, regardless of possible damage to her complexion.

Her sisters told her she was a fool to risk her looks, but she enjoyed being with her father, and actually found, although it seemed incredible, that she was bored by their long conversations about the latest fashions or, after Mirabel had been presented at Court, the gossip about the love-affairs of people she had never seen.

As Elmina was the youngest, she inevitably wore all her sisters' cast-off clothes, and as she was not yet officially a débutante, the opinions of the Social World and its fashions did not concern her.

She was just wondering now as she finished her breakfast how quickly she could slip away to the stables before her mother found some task for her to do in the house, when the Butler came into the room with a note on a silver salver.

He took it to the Earl at the end of the table saying pompously:

"This has been brought by a Groom, M'Lord. He's waiting for an answer."

The Earl glanced at the note without much interest.

"Who is it from, Barton?"

"The Marquis of Falcon, M'Lord!"

The Earl stiffened and sat upright.

"Falcon? What the devil does he want?"

"Really, George, not in front of the girls!" the Countess exclaimed. "I had no idea the Marquis was in residence."

"Neither had I," the Earl replied. "He spoke to me at White's last week, but as there was a hideous noise being made by some of the younger members, I did not actually hear what he said."

"Perhaps it is an invitation, Papa!" Deirdre suggested.

Mirabel laughed.

"That is as likely as the Marquis asking himself to luncheon! We have never been invited to Falcon in eighteen years, and we are not likely to be asked now."

The Earl took the note from the salver, opened it and then spent some time searching for his spectacles, which were not in the pocket in which he expected them to be.

When he had placed them on his nose he peered again at the letter in front of him, staring at it for such a long time that eventually his wife asked:

"What is it, George? What does the Marquis want?"

"Good God!" the Earl ejaculated. "I cannot believe it! Or else my eyes are deceiving me!"

"What has happened? What does he say?" his wife enquired.

Elmina was about to leave the table, but now curious as to what the letter contained she sat down again.

The Earl stared once more at the piece of paper he held in his hand. Then as if he were suddenly aware that not only his family but also his Butler was waiting with understandable curiosity, he said:

"I will ring, Barton. Tell the Groom to wait."

"Very good, M'Lord!"

There was just a faint note of disappointment in the elderly Butler's voice.

He had been with the family for over thirty years, and he was always eager to know what was going on as soon as, if not sooner than, it actually happened.

The Earl however waited until the Pantry door had shut behind him before he said:

"I can hardly believe this is not some joke. Falcon suggests he should marry my daughter!"

For a moment there was complete silence. Then the Countess exclaimed:

"You must be mistaken! Surely he cannot write anything like that out of the blue, without any preliminaries?"

"Now that I think about it," the Earl said heavily, "that must be what he was saying to me the other night at White's. To tell the truth, my dear, I had drunk rather a lot of port with old Anstruther, and as Falcon was also on the side of my bad ear, I just nodded and smiled at what he was saying, not realising I was agreeing to anything like this."

"I can hardly believe it!" the Countess cried.

"Personally, I consider it an insult!" Mirabel said firmly. "Thank goodness I do not have to marry him!"

"What do you mean—not marry him?" the Earl asked.

He looked at his eldest daughter as if he had never seen her before, then said slowly:

"The Falcon tiara is very becoming!"

Mirabel gave a little scream.

"What are you saying, Papa? What are you thinking? You know I intend to marry Robert, and you have already given your consent."

"Your engagement is a secret at the moment, and has not yet been announced."

Mirabel gave another scream.

"You promised, Papa! You know you promised, and no gentleman would go back on his word."

The Earl gave a little sigh and looked at his second daughter.

Deirdre had already anticipated this and she said:

"Before you say another word, Papa, I have no intention of marrying the Marquis of Falcon! I have always disliked him for the discourteous way he had treated us when we have been out hunting and in any case, although I have not told you about it, Christopher and I have an understanding."

"Christopher Bardsley!" the Countess exclaimed. "Oh, Deirdre, why did you not confide in me? I have hoped so much that he would be attracted to you."

"He is very attracted," Deirdre answered, "but it has not been possible for him to speak to Papa while his father is so desperately ill and is expected to die at any moment."

"I quite understand," the Countess said in a soft voice, "and I am sure, dearest child, you will be very happy with such a charming young man."

She was thinking as she spoke that while Christopher was handsome and had, she thought, the best manners of any young man who came to the house, his father, Lord Bardsley, who lived about fifteen miles away had a very fine Estate which Christopher would inherit with the title as soon as he died.

"Thank you, Mama," Deirdre said. "I thought you would understand. I have not spoken of it before because Christopher said it would seem heartless when his father was dying."

"That is all very well," the Earl said sharply, "but what am I to say to Falcon?"

"I will marry him, Papa!"

If Elmina had fired a pistol in the Breakfast Room, she could not have caused more surprise.

They all turned to stare at her, and the Earl said in a not very complimentary fashion:

"You? Of course he cannot marry you!"

"Why not?" Elmina asked.

"You are too young for one thing," the Countess interposed.

"I shall be eighteen next week," Elmina said, "and you must remember, Mama, that your only excuse for not presenting me at Court this Season was that you could not contemplate three girls on your hands, and that Papa would grumble at the expense."

She paused and then as nobody seemed to have anything to say she added:

"I am quite old enough to be married, and I am prepared to marry the Marquis!"

The Earl looked at his daughter as if she were a

young horse and he was considering her points.

"The question is," he said heavily after a moment, "whether the Marquis would be prepared to marry you."

"He cannot be very particular, Papa, for as far as we know, he has never noticed either Mirabel or Deirdre, so I imagine any one of your daughters would be just as acceptable as another."

The Countess drew in her breath.

"I still feel, George, that this is an insult! How can he write to you, asking to marry one of your daughters, without approaching you in the proper manner first?"

"I have just explained to you that Falcon must have approached me the other night, when I could not hear properly what he was saying to me. He has now put it in writing, and you cannot pretend he is not a man anybody would welcome as a son-in-law."

The Countess was silent.

She was thinking of the Marquis's importance in the Social World, his huge Estate which marched with theirs, his immense wealth, and the fact that in her experience everybody spoke of him with awe.

It was as if he were an inhabitant of a different Planet from the one in which they lived.

Now the Earl looked at Elmina again, as if to make sure he was not mistaken.

Then he said coaxingly to Mirabel:

"Surely, my dearest, you must realise the position you would have as the Marchioness of Falcon? Hereditary Lady-of-the-Bedchamber, *persona grata* at Court, and there is never a distinguished visitor from abroad who does not expect to be entertained at Falcon."

"Then they are more fortunate than we are! We live within five miles of the house and hear about it from everybody we meet, but never once, Papa, have we been invited to the Balls, the Garden-Parties, or even the Steeple-Chases which take place there!"

"I ride in them," the Earl said sharply.

"That is very kind of him, is it not?" Mirabel said scornfully. "He could hardly ignore you, since occasionally he hunts with your hounds! But how often has he asked you and Mama to dinner?"

There was no reply so she added:

"I cannot recall a single instance since I was old enough to notice what you did and where you were going."

The Earl was silent.

He knew that Mirabel was only saying what he himself had said a thousand times to his wife in private.

"I call it a damned insult!" he had repeated over and over again. "Falcon thinks the people who live next to him in the County are not good enough to cross his threshold."

"I suppose, darling," the Countess had said with a little sigh, having heard all this before, "the Marquis thinks we are old and boring. We cannot really blame him when he is acclaimed and run after by every Beauty in the Kingdom, and of course by every ambitious Mama!"

"Well, all I can say," the Earl growled, "is that

the father had better manners than the son!"

Whatever was said about him, the Marquis had gone his own way.

He had entertained at his enormous, magnificent house only those he wished to have as his guests, and although his neighbours ground their teeth in fury and the women bit their nails, the coveted invitations never came!

But of course news of the gaieties of the Marquis's hospitality swept towards them on the wind.

The Earl looked down again at the letter.

"Well, what are we going to do about this?" he asked.

"Let Elmina marry him, Papa, if that is what she wants," Deirdre said before anybody else could speak.

There was a little tremor in her voice which told her sisters she was terrified that her father might insist on her throwing over Christopher Bardsley, with whom she was very much in love, because a bigger fish was being dangled in front of her eyes.

"I am quite certain that when the Marquis suggested he should marry my daughter he was thinking of Mirabel," the Earl said. "After all, she had been about London, and he has doubtless seen her at the Devonshires' or the Richmonds' Balls."

"If he did see me," Mirabel said quickly, "he did not pay me the compliment of even one glance in my direction. He was, if you want to know, extremely busy with Lady Carstairs, whose grace and beauty, according to the magazines, is greater than any that has ever before graced a London Ball-Room!"

"I agree with that," the Earl said spontaneously, then caught his wife's eye.

"Come along! Come along!" he said in a loud tone. "The Groom is waiting, and I have to give His Lordship some sort of answer!"

"Tell him that you accept his proposal, Papa," Elmina said, "and invite him to luncheon or dinner—but not before the end of next week."

Her father looked at her enquiringly and she said:

"That will give me time to buy one decent gown before he meets me, which is more than I have at the moment!"

As if Elmina's words made her mother suddenly conscious of how young and untidy she looked at the moment, she said quickly:

"Please, George, do not do anything hastily. I cannot think that Elmina is a suitable wife for the Marquis of Falcon! If you accept his proposal now, it might be difficult later to retract it."

"Why should I want to do that?" the Earl asked aggressively. "The man has asked for my daughter's hand in marriage, and as I apparently have only one daughter available, it has to be Elmina!"

"But, really..." the Countess began only to be interrupted as the Earl rose from the table.

"I am going to write to Falcon, accepting his proposal. If you want the truth, I think it is damned insulting, but I am not such a fool as not to be aware of the advantages, when our Estates merge with each other's, and Falcon, by all accounts, is as rich as Croesus!"

He paused as he reached the door. Then he looked back.

"If the man is such a fool as to buy a horse without first inspecting it," he observed, "then he gets only what he deserves!"

He went from the Breakfast Room, slamming the door to behind him.

For a moment there was only silence.

Then Mirabel looked at Deirdre and said:

"Thank God Papa could not upset my engagement to Robert!"

"Or mine to Christopher!" Deirdre said. "I thought for one awful moment . . ."

"So did I!" Mirabel agreed.

The Countess had risen as her husband left and now she followed him from the room.

The three girls were alone and Deirdre said as she looked at her younger sister:

"You are very brave, Elmina! I think the Marquis is terrifying. I would rather marry the Devil himself!"

"That is an unkind thing to say," Mirabel admonished. "At the same time, Elmina, I think you will find him very difficult to manage."

"He has the most magnificent horses I have ever seen," Elmina said dreamily, "and the inside of Falcon is so beautiful that it might be a fairy-tale Palace."

"The *inside?*" Mirabel and Deirdre screamed together. "What do you mean—the *inside?* You have never been there!"

Elmina smiled.

"Yes, I have, many times!"

"But how? Why did you not tell us?"

"It was my secret. The Marquis's Head Groom once asked the Housekeeper to show me round after I had done him a favour."

"You did the Marquis's Head Groom a favour?" Mirabel repeated rather stupidly. "How can you have done anything like that?"

"It happened a few years ago," Elmina said. "I was coming back from Hunting when my horse cast a shoe. I realised because I had a long way to go home that it might make him lame unless I took him very, very slowly, and it was growing dark. Then I remembered Papa having said the Marquis had a forge at Falcon, so I went there."

"Surely that was rather pushing of you?" Mirabel remarked.

Elmina laughed.

"I was not intending to ask the Marquis himself if I could use his forge. I just rode Star into the yard, asked for the Head Groom and explained to him what had happened. He understood my plight immediately and sent for the Blacksmith, who lives in one of the houses near the stable."

She paused for a moment before she went on.

"While he was dealing with Star I talked to the man—Hogson is his name—and he told me he was having trouble poulticing some of the Marquis's horses which had been ridden by a Lady who had used her spurs unmercifully on them."

Her two sisters were listening to Elmina with rapt attention.

"You will remember," she went on, "that Papa has a special poultice which we have often used and have always been told it was invented by Grandmama, who was such a fine horsewoman. I offered to ride over the next day and give it to him."

"Why did you not tell us?"

Elmina smiled.

"As a matter of fact, I thought that Papa and Mama have always been so incensed at never being invited to Falcon that they would forbid me to keep my promise."

"Go on," Deirdre said. "What happened?"

"Hogson was very grateful, especially as the poultice was extremely effective. After he had used it he sent a message to ask me if I would give him the recipe."

"You gave him our secret recipe?" Mirabel asked. "How could you do that? You know Papa likes to think he is the only person who has it."

"Of course I did not give it to him!" Elmina replied. "I merely made up a quantity of the poultice myself and took it over. I told him it was a secret formula, but of course any time he wanted it, I would be only too willing to make it for him."

Mirabel and Deirdre gave a sigh which was one of envy.

"So that is how you got into Falcon!"

"Hogson was very grateful to me," Elmina said, "and I knew he also wanted to make certain that he could have the poultice whenever the Marquis's lady-friends ill-treated his horses. I merely remarked in an innocent sort of way that I had heard that His Lordship had the most magnificent sporting pictures, and Hogson asked if I would like to see them."

"Well, all I can say," Deirdre replied, "is that I think it was very mean of you not to have taken us with you!"

"I was well aware that Papa and Mama would have been furious at the idea of my wandering around Falcon and looking at all its glories, when they were not considered grand enough to be entertained by its owner."

"But you did not see the Marquis?" Mirabel asked quickly.

"Oh, no! I go there only when he is away. Oh, girls, you should see the Library! The Marquis has the most fantastic collection of books you could imagine! I only wish I could sit and read every one of them!"

"That is what you will be able to do if you marry him," Deirdre said.

For a moment Elmina looked startled.

"Yes, of course! I had not thought of that!"

Then she gave a little cry and said:

"But I suppose really I am marrying the Marquis for his horses. I think I know every one of them, and I cannot believe it would be possible to find a finer stable in the whole world!"

"How many times have you been to Falcon?" Mirabel asked curiously.

"Oh, lots and lots of times," Elmina answered carelessly. "When you went off to London and Mama said I was to stay behind and work at my lessons, it was the one amusement I had. It was only fair that I should enjoy myself, while you were having such a marvellous time!"

Quite suddenly her two sisters burst into laughter.

"It cannot be true! But really, Elmina, you are mean to keep such excitements to yourself!"

"You must not tell Papa or Mama!" Elmina warned. "They would, as you know, be very shocked at my being so deceitful. But seeing Falcon is like stepping into another world, and so fascinating that I somehow do not feel that it is real, but only part of my dreams."

"That is a very good excuse!" Mirabel said sarcastically. "And now you are going to marry the man of your dreams, and I only hope he will come up to your expectations. I must say, in your shoes I would be terrified!"

"It is not going to be easy, I realise that," Elmina said in a quiet voice, "but there will be the horses, and of course all those thousands of books!"

As if she did not wish her sisters to reply, Elmina turned as she finished speaking and left the room.

When she had gone Mirabel looked at Deirdre for some time before she said:

"She is too young to know what she is doing."

"Yes, I know," Deirdre agreed, "but she will find out what he is like once she is married to him."

"If you ask me, he will make her utterly and completely miserable," Mirabel said, "and we ought to stop it."

"How?" Deirdre asked. "You know Papa in fact is thrilled at the idea of having the Marquis as his son-in-law, and it will solve his financial problems, we can be quite certain of that."

"I have realised that already," Mirabel agreed, "but it is Elmina we have to think of."

"I have a shrewd suspicion that Elmina is quite capable of looking after herself," Deirdre replied. "How could she go into Falcon without telling us, when I have been yearning, ever since I was in the cradle, to have a look inside it."

"I have always thought the Marquis quite repulsive!" Mirabel said. "In the hunting-field he always puts on that supercilious air of a man condescending to associate with his inferiors."

Deirdre smiled.

"You are saying that only because he did not admire you as everybody else has!"

"I did not wish him to admire me."

Deirdre gave a sudden exclamation.

"Of course! I know now why he has proposed!"

"Why?" Mirabel asked.

"Because you are really very like Lady Carstairs! Not so beautiful, of course, but she has hair like yours and enormous blue eyes that seem to reflect the stars."

"Are my eyes like that?" Mirabel asked curiously.

"You resemble our grandmother in the picture by Sir Joshua Reynolds, and she was one of the greatest beauties of her time!"

"I know she was," Mirabel said, "and I have often thought I might try to cultivate the same blissful expression."

"It would only make you look half-witted," Deirdre said with the frankness of a sister, "and you do very well as you are. You do not really want to marry anybody except Robert?"

"No, of course not! He is wonderful," Mirabel replied. "I nearly died when I thought for one awful moment that Papa was going to make me marry the Marquis!"

"It was worse for me because I had not told him about Christopher!"

"Christopher will be a Lord," Mirabel said, "which is certainly a point in his favour, while I shall be only a Baronet's wife."

There was a pause before she added:

"But our little sister Elmina will be the Marchioness of Falcon and will walk in to dinner in front of us!"

Quite suddenly Deirdre laughed.

"I do not believe it is true!" she said. "How can Elmina possibly marry that stuck-up, conceited, over-whelming man? As a matter of fact, if you ask me, when he meets her he will back out!"

Mirabel gave a cry of horror.

"Of course he would not do that! It is inconceivable to think that a gentleman and a sportsman could be-have in such a crooked manner. At the same time, if he supposes he is marrying me, I cannot help thinking he is in for a shock which will do him a lot of good!"

"Then what we have to do is to try to help Elmina in every way we can," Deirdre said. "She is quite right: she must have some decent gowns to wear in-stead of those cut-down old garments of ours which make her look like a rag-bag."

There was a pause, then Mirabel said:

"Poor Elmina! My heart bleeds for her, and of course we must do everything in our power to help her, but I am not at all certain what that is!"

"We shall just have to try," Deirdre said.

Having left the Breakfast Room, Elmina ran as quickly as she could out to the stables.

Although she was strictly forbidden to come in to breakfast in her riding-habit, she spent so much time in the morning with the horses that she invariably disobeyed her mother's instructions and wore her habit.

In fact, she wore nothing else from the moment she got up in the morning until it was time to change for dinner in the evening.

She had therefore only to pick up her riding-hat, which was lying on a chair with her gloves and whip, as she went through the hall on her way to the stables.

First she saw one of the stable-lads, rather a stupid boy, who just touched his forelock and went on washing down the cobble-stones.

Then she went in through the first open door to find the Groom she was seeking.

He was brushing down her own horse Star and strangely enough, although he was working in an English stable, he was Chinese.

At least that was what everybody thought he was because his name was Chang, but actually, as Elmina knew, although nobody else was interested, his mother had been Japanese and his father Dutch.

It was his grandfather who had been Chinese and from him he had inherited his eyes and his dark hair.

The story of how he came to be working in the service of the Earl was as unusual as the circumstances of how Elmina had found her way to Falcon.

21

Last year after Mirabel had been in London for two months enjoying her first Season, Deirdre, who was not to make her debut until this April, and Elmina, who was still in the School-Room, had joined their parents at their London house.

Because Deirdre was to be allowed to attend some of the Winter Balls, she was permitted to dine downstairs when there was a dinner-party in the house and drive in Rotten Row with her mother.

Elmina was however kept out of sight and either ate her meals alone, or with some of the visiting teachers who gave her special lessons while she was in London.

She had no difficulty in persuading her mother it was important for her to visit the Museums and the sights of London accompanied by one of the elderly housemaids.

One day when she was returning home, insisting because she needed the exercise on walking, much to the dismay of her companion, they came upon a road-sweeper at the crossing of a road.

Elmina noticed that he limped and because there was something about him which touched her heart she stopped and felt in her purse for a penny to give him.

As he took it he said:

"Thank you, Lady, that were a fine horse you were riding in the Park this morning!"

Elmina looked at him in surprise and while she thought his face looked strange she answered:

"I am glad you think so! My father has just bought him and I think when he is a little older he will be quite exceptional!"

"I'm sure of it, Lady," the man said, "but tell that young lad who rides him not to keep him on such a tight rein. His mouth's tender, and if you look closely you'll see that it's sore!"

Elmina looked at him in surprise.

"How do you know this?" she asked.

"I look at all the horses around here," the man said simply.

"If you like horses so much, why are you sweeping the road?"

She knew as she asked it that it was a silly question.

"I was thrown and broke m'leg," the man replied. "But it were badly mended, and now one leg's shorter than th'other."

He gave a sigh as he said:

"It doesn't prevent me riding, but nobody wants a crippled man in their stable!"

There was so much feeling in his voice that Elmina said:

"My father's Head Groom was telling me this morning that he is looking for another stable-boy. Come with me, and we will see if you could fill the post."

There was a sudden light in the slanting eyes looking at her as the man said:

"May good fortune walk beside you all the days of your life!"

She felt that he was translating from his own language into English and she was also well aware that he spoke in a far more educated manner than any Englishman in similar circumstances would have.

Regardless of the muttered protests of the housemaid who chaperoned her, Elmina took the man, who told her his name was Chang, round to the Mews.

The Earl's Head Groom had for years found how useful Elmina was in helping him to look after the horses.

He was not prepared therefore to oppose her in anything she suggested, but he felt slightly apprehensive in case he was doing the wrong thing.

He agreed however to give Chang a try, and from that moment on Chang had made himself indispensable.

Only gradually had he related to Elmina some of his strange history.

He had travelled all over the world in one capacity or another, as a Courier to rich merchants going East and with gentlemen going on Big Game shoots.

He had served on a Merchant Ship and, as he said with a touch of pride in his voice, had 'ridden everything from a yak to an elephant!'

When the Earl and Countess returned to the country, there was no question but that Chang should go with them.

At Warne Park, once the other servants got used to his strange appearance, he seemed to fit in in any capacity that was required of him.

If the Earl's valet was ill, he took his place; if they were short of a footman, he helped wait at table; if anything unusual was wanted, Chang provided it.

Whatever time of the day or night, if anybody visited the stables, Chang always seemed to be there.

Now, as Elmina went into the first stall and Star nuzzled up to her as she patted his neck she said:

"Listen, Chang, I want your help."

He grinned at her and his thin lips seemed to stretch across his face from ear to ear.

"You've only to ask, M'Lady!"

Elmina drew in her breath.

"I am to . . . m-marry the Marquis of Falcon."

For a moment Chang's hand holding the brush was still. Then he said:

"His Lordship's got some fine horses!"

"Very fine! But I want you to tell me what you think of him as a man."

She did not have to remind Chang that they had discussed the Marquis before, when they had seen him in the Hunting-Field.

They had also watched, although neither the Earl nor the Countess were aware of it, two Steeple-Chases in the grounds of Falcon.

They were exciting races in which the Marquis's younger friends had taken part, but to which the Earl had not been invited.

Elmina had thought then that no man could ride better than the Marquis or seem so much a part of his horse.

At the same time she had been aware that the contests were unfair in that the Marquis was not only the best rider, but also had the best horses.

It was obvious he would win, and she and Chang had lain flat on the grass on the rising ground above one point of the race-course, watching the competitors taking the fences beneath them.

They had criticised their style, the way they handled their horses and their appearance.

Only where the Marquis was concerned had they made no comments, and yet Elmina had felt that Chang thought a great many things that he had not said.

She had grown so fond of the strange little man she had introduced into the household that he had become her only confidant and in many ways her guide.

She found, and it had not surprised her, that Chang had studied the teaching of Confucius, as well as other Eastern religions, although she was not certain to which he actually belonged.

She felt too that he used what were almost mystical powers when he dealt with the difficult horses, which would then do anything he wanted of them, and also when he was dealing with people.

She had always been certain that he had deliberately evoked her interest in him when she stopped to give him a penny, simply because some inner sense had told him she would be able to help him when everybody else had failed to do so.

Now she asked him simply and without any embarrassment to tell her about the man she was to marry.

She waited in silence for nearly a minute before Chang said in the voice he used when he was looking as she described to herself as 'inwards.'

Then he said:

"His Lordship's a man who has great possibilities, M'Lady. But everything comes to him too easily. He's only to want—and it's there! As they say in China: 'He holds out his hand, and the peach falls!' That's not good. A man must fight for what he wants, not

26

with his body, but with his mind, and it's his instinct to be a hunter!"

"Thank you, Chang. That has been a help, and now it is important that I should work at my Ju Jitsu. We have been slack about it lately, and I have not had a lesson for two weeks."

"Very good, M'Lady. What time you wish me to be upstairs?"

Elmina calculated that her mother would, as usual, go and rest before dinner at five o'clock and she was certain her sisters would be writing to the men with whom they were in love to tell them what had happened.

"I will be ready at five-thirty, Chang," she said. "That will give us over an hour before I have my bath."

"Very good, M'Lady."

"I expect Papa will want to ride in about twenty minutes."

She thought it would take her father all that time to compose a note to the Marquis, and doubtless he would make various attempts at it before he was satisfied.

"Which horse will His Lordship ride?" Chang enquired.

"I think both Papa and I will need a challenge," Elmina said with a smile. "Saddle those two new horses we are breaking in. They will give us no time to think or talk about anything else."

Chang grinned.

Then having kissed Star lightly on his nose, Elmina

hurried back to the Hall to wait patiently for her father.

Having handed over to Barton his letter for the Marquis, he came towards her scowling, because he had a feeling that things were happening that he did not understand.

He was, in fact, not certain whether he was pleased or insulted by the Marquis of Falcon's high-handed behaviour.

chapter two

"THE Marquis of Falcon, M'Lady!" the Butler announced.

Lady Carstairs gave a well-simulated cry of surprise, and as the door closed behind the servant she ran across the Drawing-Room floor with both her hands outstretched.

"Alston, my dear!" she exclaimed. "I was so worried when I heard you had gone to the country, but you are back!"

"Yes, I am back," the Marquis said in the slow, drawling tone that was characteristic of him.

He kissed each of the outstretched hands extended to him but ignored the invitation of two red lips, and moved across the room to stand with his back to the fireplace.

Lady Carstairs eyed him a little warily.

She thought it was strange that he had not taken her into his arms, but she was too experienced in the ways of men to make any comment.

Instead she moved slowly and sinuously to join him at the fireplace, aware that the gown she was wearing clung to her figure in all the right places, and it would be impossible for any man not to admire the curves of her body as well as the beauty of her face.

."How could you have gone away without telling me?" she asked in a soft voice which invariably evoked a protective response in her admirers.

"I had some horses arriving at Falcon," the Marquis replied, "and I wished to ensure that they were correctly stabled and were as good as they looked when I bought them."

"I am sure they are perfect, as is everything you possess!" Lady Carstairs said. "And I hope there are some superlative ones with which you will allow me to drive in the Park."

The Marquis noted that she said 'drive' and not 'ride,' knowing that Lady Carstairs was not really happy on a horse.

Although occasionally she appeared on horseback, it was only to show off her riding-habits, which were smarter than those most other women wore and she also liked to have a posse of men riding with her.

Instead of answering her question as she expected, the Marquis said:

"I have something to tell you, Sapphire."

It was a name he always found difficulty in remembering, because he was well aware that Lady Carstairs had been christened 'Sarah.'

But finding when she was a reigning beauty it was too common-place a name, she had changed it to Sapphire simply because she owned a particularly fine necklace of the stones.

There was a note in his voice that seemed, although Lady Carstairs was not certain, somewhat unusual.

Clasping her hands together a little theatrically, she asked:

"Oh, Alston, what is it? There is not any trouble—I hope?"

"That depends upon what you call 'trouble,'" the Marquis replied. "The fact is I am going to be married!"

He spoke bluntly, almost as if he felt it was best to get the matter over and had no intention of leaking out the truth slowly to make it more palatable.

There was a perceptible pause before Lady Carstairs repeated almost beneath her breath:

"Married?"

Raising her large blue eyes up to his, she asked:

"But, why—and to whom? Why have I not—heard of this—before?"

Her voice gradually rose until as she said the last word she was almost shrieking, and the Marquis said quickly:

"It is something I have trying to avoid for some time, Sapphire, although I knew it would have to happen sooner or later because it is necessary for me to have an heir."

"Of course, of course!" Lady Carstairs agreed. "But why now—just when we are so—happy?"

There was a tremor on the word 'happy' as if she

might burst into tears, and the Marquis said:

"I will tell you the reason. Then you will understand that there is no need for hysterics or to make a fuss over what is an entirely natural occurrence."

"It is not—natural to—me!" Lady Carstairs objected.

She sat down on the edge of the sofa as she spoke, and drawing a small lace-edged handkerchief from the belt of her gown, lifted it to her eyes.

The Marquis knew that if there were any tears, she would not allow them to fall or brush them away, when the tips of her long eye-lashes that were as gold as her hair, had been darkened with mascara.

"The explanation is quite simple," he said in a lofty tone, "and actually in the circumstances you will find no reason to be jealous."

"Of course I am jealous!" Lady Carstairs interrupted. "I love you, Alston, as you well know, as I have never loved any man in my whole life before! How can you do—this to—me?"

"What is more to the point, I am doing it to myself!" the Marquis said with a somewhat wry twist of his lips. "Let me make it quite clear, Sapphire, I have no wish to marry! In fact, if you want the truth, it is a damned nuisance!"

"Then why are you to be married?"

"You can blame the Queen for that!"

"The Queen?"

There was a different note in Lady Carstairs's voice now.

Then after a second's silence she said:

"You are not saying—you are not suggesting that

the Queen—knows about us?"

"I expect so," the Marquis replied perfunctorily, "although I doubt if the Prime Minister would have told her."

"Do you mean to tell me that Lord John Russell is involved in this?"

"Yes, I do!" the Marquis replied. "In actual fact it was he who suggested I should be married!"

Lady Carstairs made a sound that was one of disgust.

"How dare he interfere! How dare he concern himself with matters which are outside his jurisdiction!"

"That is where you are wrong," the Marquis said, "and if you will stop talking for a moment, Sapphire, I will tell you exactly what has happened."

Lady Carstairs gave what purported to be a heart-rending sob before she said:

"I cannot—bear it! How can I bear to—think of you—married to—anybody but me?"

"That is somewhat of an impossibility, unless you are prepared to be bigamous!" the Marquis said dryly.

"Oh, Alston, how can you be so unkind when you know you have broken my heart?"

"I have done nothing of the sort!" he retorted with just a touch of irritation in his voice. "Now, if you will only listen to the truth, you will understand."

"I am—listening!" Lady Carstairs faltered.

"Russell sent for me last week," the Marquis began, "and informed me I was the man who was far the most suited to become Master of the Horse to Her Majesty!"

Lady Carstairs looked up and exclaimed:

"Of course! How could anybody be as good or as knowledgeable as you in that particular post?"

"But His Lordship also said," the Marquis went on as if she had not interrupted, "that both he and Her Majesty thought it advisable that the position should be filled by a married man!"

Lady Carstairs did not speak, but the Marquis knew she was beginning to understand as he continued.

"Russell suggested with all the tact for which he is famous that I was really too young to be Master of the Horse unless I was married, and he even insinuated that otherwise the Prince Consort might be jealous of me!"

"That does not surprise me," Lady Carstairs remarked, almost as if she knew it was her cue to say something flattering.

"Considering the Queen is besotted by her stiff and boring husband," the Marquis said, "and thinks the sun rises and sets on him, I should hardly have thought there was room for me!"

"Any woman from the Queen to a milk-maid would fall in love with you, dearest Alston, at first sight!" Lady Carstairs declared. "But are you saying that you really have to go to such lengths as to be married?"

"I will tell you quite frankly that I do want to be Master of the Horse. The Royal Stables are in a disgraceful state since King William was never particularly interested in horse-flesh and, although the Prince Consort has tightened up and improved the inside of the Palace, he is nevertheless an ignoramus when it comes to horses!"

There was a glint in the Marquis's eyes as he spoke,

as if he were looking forward to the task of sweeping away what he privately thought of as the 'dust and rubbish of ages.'

Because she felt he had not yet given her the most important information of all, Lady Carstairs asked faintly:

"Who is this—fortunate girl who is to marry the most—attractive man in—the whole world?"

"That is the question I have been asking myself," the Marquis said. "I do not mind telling you, Sapphire, that I had great difficulty in finding an answer."

He gave a short laugh.

"After all, in the life I lead I do not come in contact with marriageable young women, but only with lovely creatures like yourself!"

He looked down at Lady Carstairs as he spoke, and as if he found her beauty very appealing, his hard eyes softened for a moment.

"You are very beautiful, Sapphire!" he said. "So I knew it would be hopeless to look for anybody half as lovely as you."

"Oh, Alston, if only I could marry you myself! Perhaps..."

She hesitated.

"I saw Carstairs the day before I left," the Marquis interrupted, "and he appeared to be in the finest of health. In fact he told me he was leaving tomorrow to attend the race-meeting at Doncaster."

"So that is why you came back!"

Lady Carstairs sprang to her feet and moved towards the Marquis.

He put his arms around her, then looking down at

the beautiful face turned up to his, he scrutinised it for a long moment before he kissed her.

As he did so she pressed herself closer and closer against him, and their kiss became more passionate, until the Marquis made the first move and deliberately set her on one side.

"Now, listen, Sapphire," he said, "because I have a great many important things to do, having been out of London for three days."

"But we will dine together tomorrow night?" she asked.

"Yes, of course."

"Oh, Alston, it seems a very long time away!"

"I know," he replied, "but you must be very careful not to get talked about unnecessarily. You know how spiteful people are, and I do not wish them to gossip about us at Buckingham Palace, or in the country for that matter."

"I will be very, very careful," Lady Carstairs promised, "but I love you and when you are there it is difficult for me to think of anything else, or to know that there is any other person in the room!"

The Marquis had heard this too often for it to come as a novel declaration.

Instead he merely kissed Lady Carstairs again and said:

"I must leave you. I expect your husband will be back soon, and this is not a moment for him to be kicking up a fuss!"

"I am sure he would do nothing of the sort!" Lady Carstairs said almost indignantly.

The Marquis was not listening.

"Take care of yourself," he said. "I will expect you at seven-thirty tomorrow night."

He paused, then said:

"I suppose it would be more sensible if I invited a few other people to dine as well."

"Oh, no, Alston!" Lady Carstairs exclaimed. "No! No! I want to be alone with you!"

"Well, perhaps we will be able to make some other sort of arrangement in the future," the Marquis said as if he were speaking to himself.

She went close to him and he held her for a moment before he put her aside preparatory to leaving the room.

It was then as she quickly collected her scattered senses that she said:

"You must promise me, Alston, on everything you hold Holy, that you will not let this horrible marriage of yours make—any difference to—us!"

Her voice sharpened as she went on.

"How could I lose you? How can I bear to be without you? Oh, dearest, wonderful Alston, no woman has ever had such a perfect lover as you, and I would rather die than live without you!"

This again was what the Marquis had heard too often for it to make any particular impact on him.

Instead he merely said:

"We will talk about it tomorrow night."

Only as he took the first step towards the door did Lady Carstairs say, "But Alston, you have not yet told me whom you are to marry! Do I know her?"

"You may have seen her at one of the Balls you have attended," the Marquis said vaguely. "She is the

Earl of Warnborough's daughter, whose estate marches with mine."

Lady Carstairs looked blank.

"I cannot remember ever meeting a girl called Warnborough!"

"Warne!" the Marquis corrected. "And I am told she is very pretty!"

"You are—told? Are you saying you have not yet met her?"

"Not to my knowledge. I would have done so this week if I had not received your letter telling me that you would be alone."

"Yes, alone, dearest, except for you, and I know how wonderful it will be!"

The Marquis smiled at her. Then he said briskly;

"I really must go. I shall be late anyway, which is a mistake!"

"Where are you going?" Lady Carstairs enquired curiously.

"To the Palace," the Marquis replied. "But I have to see Russell first in Downing Street to inform him that I am now completely eligible to be Master of the Horse."

He did not wait for Lady Carstairs's answer but went from the room before her clinging hands could delay him.

As he walked down the stairs he thought with satisfaction that the interview had passed off much less uncomfortably than he had anticipated.

He was well aware that all women in whom he took an interest became immediately over-possessive.

It was something he disliked, but it was unfortunately something he could not control.

It usually arose when they suspected or learnt that there was another woman involved, together with tears and recriminations and wild assertions that if they lost his love, they would kill themselves.

As none of them had ever done so, and he had over and over again heard the threat repeated, he knew cynically that however much their hearts might seem to be involved, the Beauties with whom he spent his time had a real affection only for themselves.

Nevertheless, there was nothing he disliked more than a scene such as he had just avoided with considerable dexterity.

It had, he told himself complacently, been quite a stroke of genius to tell Sapphire he had not even met the girl he was to marry, for even she would find it difficult to be jealous of somebody who was faceless.

He often thought that the women to whom he made love and who found him so attractive were very lucky that he was not married already.

Most men in his position had been marched up the aisle as the result of continual pressure from their parents, before they had the good sense or the strength or will to speak up for themselves.

In his case he had come into the title when he was only nineteen and had from that moment been his own master and obliged to answer to no one.

He had therefore found his life entrancing where women were concerned so that he had no intention of marrying until the last possible moment, although there had been times when he had had to fight very hard to remain a bachelor.

This was, of course, against women who had been widowed, for he had never at any time been so foolish as to show any interest in an unmarried girl.

He knew that to do so would be tantamount to proclaiming an interest in her, with marriage at least possible in view.

However when Lord John Russell told him what was expected, he had thought that to be Master of the Horse might compensate for what he was certain would inevitably be the complete and utter boredom of being married.

His wife would be an unfledged, gauche young woman with whom he had no interests in common, except that she would give him a son and heir.

But his common sense told him that he had to marry sooner or later, and if the pill was to be sugared by the horses from the Royal Stables, then it would not be so hard to swallow as it might otherwise have been.

He had therefore searched his memory to think when he had seen any attractive young women at any of the Balls and parties he attended almost nightly.

He then discovered that the only unmarried girls he could recall had been the Ladies-in-Waiting to the young Queen.

It was not only that they were an uncommonly plain lot, but he also had no intention of becoming too closely involved with the Queen and the Prince Consort's intimate circle.

He had already found that the evenings he had

spent, which were as few as possible, at Buckingham Palace, were extremely dull, and he had no wish to add to them because his wife held a position at Court.

"One of us is quite enough!" he told himself.

He knew that at the back of his mind he had always had the idea that when he was married, his wife would stay at Falcon and not come to London more than was absolutely necessary.

Despairing of finding a solution, he had taken one of his closest friends into his confidence.

Major Charles Marriott was in the Horse Guards.

He agreed immediately that there was nobody in the whole Kingdom more suited to be appointed Master of the Horse, but added that the idea of his having to marry in order to attain such a position horrified him.

"You have always hated the idea of being married, Alston," he said, "and you know as well as I do that even the most scintillating Beauty palls on you after a month or so. How then could you stand being tied to one woman for the rest of your life?"

"There is no alternative," the Marquis said briefly. "Now, come on, Charles, be constructive! You must know some girls!"

"Not if I can help it!" Charles Marriott replied. "No—wait a minute!"

He put his fingers up to his forehead as if to help himself to think, then said:

"There was one rather pretty girl I noticed last Season. As a matter of fact she rather reminded me of Sapphire Carstairs."

"You mean she looked like her?"

"A pale reflection."

"What was her name?"

"I am trying to remember! Oh, yes! She is the daughter of Warnborough, whom we often see at White's. You know, the red-faced man. I think you said he was a neighbour of yours."

"The Earl of Warnborough!" the Marquis exclaimed. "His Estates march with mine."

"There you are then," Charles Marriott said, "what could be more convenient? At least you know what stable she has come out of, and there will be no unpleasant surprises to be unearthed after you are married."

"It is certainly an idea," the Marquis agreed. "Actually, I rather like Warnborough. He rides well, in fact very well, and is Master of the pack with which I hunt occasionally, when it is too much trouble to go farther afield."

"Then that problem is solved!" Charles Marriott said. "I suppose we had better have a drink on it!"

A few days later the Marquis had seen the Earl of Warnborough at White's Club and thought it a good opportunity to suggest that as their lands were adjoining, their families might be closer.

He had phrased it, he thought, tactfully and with a certain amount of elegance, and the Earl had smiled and nodded his approval.

It was two days later before he remembered he ought also to confirm the proposition in writing.

The Earl's reply, which his Groom brought back

to him from Warne Park, had been exactly what he had expected.

He therefore sent the Earl another letter saying that as he unfortunately had to return to London immediately, he would be delighted to dine at Warne Park in two weeks' time and in return perhaps the Earl would bring his wife and daughter to dinner at Falcon a few days later.

He had gone back to London with the comfortable feeling that he had done his duty, and there could now be nothing to prevent the Queen from appointing him as Master of the Horse almost immediately.

It did not strike him until he found the note waiting for him at Falcon House in Park Lane that Sapphire Carstairs might be upset!

Then he realised there was another hurdle to be jumped before he was, as he put it to himself, 'galloping down the straight.'

Now, it having turned out better than he had dared to hope, he went off with a great feeling of satisfaction to see the Prime Minister, wondering how much money he would be permitted to spend on making the alterations to the Royal Mews that were urgently needed.

He also wanted to restock what was, in his opinion, a stable that was not worthy of a small City tradesman, let alone a reigning Monarch.

*   *   *

Left alone, Lady Carstairs had at first thought despairingly that when the Marquis married she might lose him.

Then she told herself sensibly that she herself was married and it need make little or no difference to her relationship.

She thought that if the Marquis's wife was a young and unsophisticated girl, it would be far easier for him to keep her in ignorance than if she were a contemporary.

"It will be all right—I know it will be all right!" she told herself, staring at her reflection in the mirror and feeling with satisfaction, it would be impossible for any woman to be lovelier than she was.

At the same time it was infuriating to think that as the Marchioness of Falcon, some insignificant chit would wear the fantastic jewels she had always coveted, sit at the end of the table in the Baronial Dining-Room at Falcon, and be hostess at the Marquis's parties.

It was a position she had been able to occupy when on the last few occasions she had stayed at Falcon.

"I shall hate her!" Sapphire Carstairs told her reflection in the glass.

He blue eyes flashed back at her, her lips assuming a downward slant which was very unbecoming. Then suddenly she smiled and added:

"At the same time I would be charming to her and make myself her friend! That will ensure that she will be only too eager to have me advise her in London and in the country, and of course, she will want me to help her in everything she does, so that I shall see more of Alston than I would do otherwise!"

It was clever thinking and Sapphire Carstairs was very pleased with herself for being so intelligent.

She had always heard that when a woman was thought to be very beautiful she was supposed, at the same time, to be brainless, but she prided herself on being intelligent in many ways that were beyond the comprehension of other women.

Actually what she had was a shrewdness and a genius for self-preservation.

She had in fact, before her marriage, been of no particular importance.

Her father was a widower, the owner of a small country Estate, and had just sufficient money to be able to entertain for his débutante daughter the year she was presented at Court.

Although he had always considered Sarah very lovely because she resembled her beautiful mother with whom he had been very much in love, he had not been prepared for the furor she created when she appeared in the Social World.

With the admiration and acclamation of their friends she blossomed like a rose and within a month was talked about as being the most beautiful girl in England.

Lord Carstairs, whose first wife had died in childbirth, was a staid man of thirty-eight, who had been swept off his feet at the sight of her, and despite the difference in their ages, had persuaded Sarah's father that they should be married.

It was undoubtedly a far more brilliant marriage than Sarah or any of her relatives might have hoped for, and she therefore became a bride at the end of her first Season.

From that moment she had set out to captivate not

only the Social World in which she appeared as a débutante, but in the far more important and more sophisticated one of people who entertained each other in the great houses of London.

Before his marriage to Sarah, Lord Carstairs had as a bachelor a somewhat limited entree to this world, but now every door was open to them both.

Somebody had once said cynically that to be of importance in English society a man had to be titled and rich. He had not added that all a woman needed was to be beautiful, but that was the truth.

Beauty was the passport to every party, every Ball, every Reception and Assembly, culminating even in Buckingham Palace itself.

To Sarah Carstairs it had all the entrancement of stepping into a fairytale.

Only after five years of marriage did she begin to realise that some of the men who paid her very fulsome compliments when she danced with them made her heart beat quicker than her husband had been able to do.

When she took her first lover she was terrified, but after several more she no longer felt guilty about it and grew astute at keeping Edward in happy ignorance.

Only when she met the Marquis did she find it difficult to think of anybody else, or even to remember that she was in fact a married woman.

He filled her whole thoughts every moment of the day and she went to sleep dreaming of him.

It was not only that he was the best-looking and most fascinating man she had ever met, but he also showed her an even more glittering, glamorous world than she had seen hitherto.

His possessions and his whole background were, in her opinion as well as in that of a great many other people, far finer than anything to be found in the Royal Palaces.

But perhaps the most irresistible attraction about the Marquis which intrigued her in a way it was difficult to describe, and had intrigued a number of women before her, was his unpredictability.

No woman could ever be sure when she saw him today whether she would see him tomorrow.

No woman, whoever she was, had been able to capture him completely so that she could say he was hers.

A hundred women had cried helplessly for him, as if he were as far out of reach as the moon.

"He is mine! He is mine!" Sapphire said now to herself.

But she knew as she spoke that it was not true, and however reasonable he had made it appear on the surface, the idea of the Marquis being married was a sudden menace that she had not expected.

* * *

When Elmina learnt that the Marquis had been obliged to leave for London and would not be returning to the country for a fortnight, she heaved a sigh of relief.

This certainly gave her more time to get some decent clothes and also prepare herself for what she thought would be a series of high jumps over which she had to leap with an expertise in which she was far from feeling confident.

She passed the days thinking of the times she had seen the Marquis in the Hunting-Field, thinking of Falcon, of his horses, and telling herself it could not be true that he had agreed to marry her.

She did not underestimate the shock it might be when he realised she was not Mirabel, and yet she appreciated her father's remark that any man who bought a horse without seeing it deserved all he got.

That however would be a poor consolation if the Marquis disliked her on sight and said firmly he had been deceived into thinking she was her sister.

The only reasonable way he could explain this would be to assert that he had seen Mirabel in London and admired her from a distance, but according to her sister their paths had never crossed.

"What I have to do is to make him at least like me as I am," Elmina said to herself.

She had the feeling it was going to be a very hard task.

When she was riding with her father they deliberately did not talk of the Marquis but of what was required on the Estate.

In fact, at the back of both their minds was the thought that, if the Marquis was their neighbour and looked favourably on his new in-laws, it would be easy for him to help in many ways with problems that at the moment were heavy burdens on the Earl's exchequer.

It was not merely a question of money; it would be a matter rather of exchange perhaps of stallions for breeding mares; for the Marquis's bulls which were the finest in the country to serve the Earl's cows.

They would also share in other ways, such as implements for the farms, like threshing-machines and ploughs, and their labourers could assist one another with the harvest.

"In fact," Elmina said to herself, "our marriage could open the flood-gates of benefit for Papa if only the Marquis and I can get on with each other."

At the same time she told herself she wanted far more than that.

She had never seen another man who equalled the Marquis or in any way lived up to her ideals as he did.

She had never been very impressed with the young men who had pursued her sister Mirabel when she was at home or in London. Except of course for Robert, whom Elmina had liked on sight, and thought Mirabel would be extremely stupid if she did not fall in love with him.

All the other men had seemed effete and foolish. Many of them did not ride as well as she expected of them and knew little or nothing about horses, which inevitably made her despise them.

"How can a man use a horse to convey him from place to place without being interested in his breeding, his training and above all the way he is stabled?" she asked her father angrily when she thought one of their guests was being unnecessarily severe with the horse he was riding.

"You are setting too high a standard, my dear," the Earl remarked.

"I cannot help judging everybody else by your standards, Papa," Elmina replied. "You are an outstanding rider, everybody says so, and at the same time you love your horses and look after them."

The Earl had laughed.

"I think the truth is that you look after them for me, and if I am remiss in anything that concerns my stables, I am quite certain you would rapidly take me to task!"

"Everything I know is that you have taught me," Elmina argued.

She knew it was a compliment which her father appreciated.

She thought later in the day however as she went upstairs to the attic that the person from whom she had learnt most, in fact, was Chang.

He had taught her so much about the handling of horses that, although she had been extremely good with them before, now she knew there was really no horse in the world she could not manage if she determined to.

He had also taught her, although her parents would have been astonished and perhaps horrified if they had known, the art of Ju Jitsu and Karate.

He had never spoken of it because, as he told her later, it was something of which a man who was proficient never boasted.

But she had chanced to come to the stables one evening late and seen Chang being threatened by a visiting tradesman who was very drunk.

He had arrived with a parcel, having driven his horse for some miles at break-neck speed.

The poor animal was sweating and was almost too exhausted to make the return journey when he got into the cart.

He started thrashing the horse unmercifully, when Chang intervened.

The man, who was tall and a large burly chap, got down onto the ground, and reversing his whip so that the thick end was like a club in his hand, was ready to attack Chang with it.

The moment Elmina appeared she saw with horror how small Chang looked by comparison, and how large and menacing his opponent was.

She was a little distance from them and ready to run forward to try to stop them when to her astonishment, as the drunken man tried to strike Chang on the head with the blunt end of the whip-handle, he suddenly seemed almost to fly backwards in the air, and then crash to the ground.

For a moment Elmina thought that Chang had not moved.

Then she realised that with his leg straight as an iron bar he had struck his opponent with his foot and the force of it had carried him about six feet from him, and left him sprawling on the ground.

As she watched, Chang walked towards him, and taking the whip from his hand, broke it in two.

Then as the man seemed almost incapable of getting up, he helped him to his feet and into the cart.

Then Chang had gone to the head of the tired and frightened horse, patted him and talked to him before sternly telling the driver to take the animal easy and had sent a very chastened man out of the yard.

"How did you do that?" Elmina had asked.

Chang smiled at the astonishment on her face.

"It is Karate, M'Lady."

"What is that? Tell me!" Elmina begged.

That was the beginning.

It was, in fact, not only the beginning of learning how to defend herself, should the need arise, but a new way of thinking.

It was Chang who explained to her that bare-handed fighting had been developed in both India and China before the Bodhidharma first arrived in China in A.D. 520.

She was obviously so interested that he went on to explain how this Indian monk was the third child of the King and a brilliant student of Zen. He had created a Temple where monks were taught a special breathing technique which was the basis of a legendary system of weaponless fighting and mental concentration.

From Chang she learnt how the Buddhists inspired Kung Fu and how for centuries the monks in China and Japan had studied Kempo.

It all fascinated her and she too wanted to learn how to fight if it was necessary, and Chang was only too willing to teach her.

Eventually they found a way to do this without anybody being aware of it.

Because the house was so large the Earl and Countess had fifteen years ago closed the top floor.

It consisted of small and uncomfortable attics where previously the servants had slept, and it was quite easy to bring the housemaids down one floor, the

Nurseries a floor lower, and the men-servants were accommodated on the Ground Floor near to the Pantry.

No one ever went up to the top attics now and it was therefore easy for Chang to sweep out one of the largest, and bring up there a number of old mattresses on which when she fell, Elmina would not hurt herself.

Elmina found in a forgotten cupboard a pair of long black hose-pipe pantaloons her father had worn when he was young.

They had been invented by George IV when he was Prince Regent, and made of some close-fitting woollen material that clung to her legs and hips.

She made herself a tunic like Chang's from a piece of black satin her mother had thrown away.

The wearing of these two garments made it easy for her to execute all the movements of Karate, although the Countess would have been horrified if she had seen her.

Elmina and Chang spent many hours alone with nobody having the least idea what they were doing, until he could say with satisfaction that she was now a more than proficient pupil. She was able to take care of herself and it would be difficult for anybody to attack her successfully.

She was also just as interested now as she had been at the beginning in what lay behind one of the most interesting and fascinating ways of thought known only to the East.

From Chang she learnt a great deal about Buddhism, and followed it up by reading books on it that she either found in the library at Warne Park, or else had sent from London.

From Chang she learnt to understand Zen and also the philosophy of Confucius.

It was from Chang too that she learnt to believe in her Karma as he had always believed in his.

It was a strange study for a girl not yet eighteen.

As she went up the unused back stairs to the attic, carrying her black pantaloons and tunic in her arms, she was thinking that everything she learned from Chang was undoubtedly a part of her Karma.

It too was connected in some way she could not understand with her marriage to the Marquis of Falcon.

chapter three

THE Marquis arrived back at Falcon in an extremely good mood.

He had been appointed Master of the Horse, and the Queen had congratulated him on his forthcoming marriage.

He had also been promised quite a large sum of money towards renovating the Royal Mews, and had already decided which horses could be dispensed with when he brought in new stock.

These would be animals which he felt worthy of the part they would play both in carrying the Queen when she rode, and also appearing at State functions.

It had taken up a lot of his time and his interest, and Sapphire Carstairs had complained that he was neglecting her.

"I am not doing that," he replied. "But I have a

great deal to do and you must understand that when there is work to be done, a woman must take second place."

Lady Carstairs could have cried out in fury at so blunt a statement, but she managed just to ask:

"How can you say anything so unkind, so hateful, when I think of you from first thing in the morning—and of course all night, when you are not with me?"

Her voice was soft and beguiling, and as it was exactly what the Marquis had expected her to say, he did not consider it to be of any momentous importance.

Instead, as her husband was away for another night, he made her rapturously happy until he left her just as dawn was breaking.

She would have been extremely piqued if she had known that walking back to his own house, which was only two streets away, the Marquis was not thinking of her, but once again of his horses.

He was remembering that tomorrow, or rather today, he was going down to Falcon to see those he had recently bought for himself.

He did not remember until he was actually passing his lodgings that he was dining that evening with the Earl of Warnborough to meet his future wife.

When he recalled it, it struck him as being a bore, for he would rather be at home, where he had a great many plans to make.

It had, however, been arranged by a number of notes being passed backwards and forwards between the Earl and himself.

Now he felt that as soon as the whole thing was

settled and the date for the wedding arranged, he could put that behind him and concentrate on the Royal Mews, which was far more important.

The Marquis would not have been surprised if he had known of the flutter and agitation that was taking place at Warne Park because of his arrival.

The Countess had seen the Cook a dozen times and changed the menu every time she talked to her.

Mrs. Oliver had been in the Kitchen for over twenty years and had already decided what the party would eat for dinner, so she merely agreed with her mistress each time she was approached.

She then continued to prepare what she had decided was right in the first place.

The Countess had sent to London for several gowns for Elmina, saying that she would have to make do with them until they knew the date of the wedding, when she would take her to London to buy her trousseau.

She did not say so, but the way she fussed told Elmina all too clearly that she was aware her daughter would have to compete in appearance with the beautiful women with whom the Marquis had spent his time up until now.

Elmina had already faced this problem herself and knew far more about the Marquis's normal feminine company than her father or her mother realised.

In the countryside, as the Marquis was the most important as well as the most exciting man in the entire neighbourhood, it was inevitable that everybody would discuss him.

Not only their neighbours, but also the villagers,

and the people who worked on the estate talked incessantly about him, and everything he said or did flew as if on wings from ear to ear.

As it happened, the Countess's lady's-maid who had been with her for some years was related to the Butler at Falcon.

On her days off she regularly visited the Butler's mother, who lived in one of the Marquis's lodges, and who was, as Elmina knew, the greatest gossip in the village.

She therefore learned a great deal from her mother's lady's-maid, and more when she visited Falcon, as she did immediately after she learnt that the Marquis had left for London.

Because it was impossible for anything to take place without the servants being aware of it, she knew by the expression on Hogson's face as soon as she walked into the stables that he was aware that the Marquis was to marry her.

He might have overheard a conversation that the Marquis had with somebody else, or else his valet, who travelled with him, brought back tit-bits of what was happening in London.

Alternatively he may have thought it strange that the Grooms were continually taking notes to Warne Park and simply put two-and-two together.

Whatever the explanation of his knowledge, Elmina was aware of it.

As she went as usual from stall to stall, admiring the new horses and making a fuss of those with whom she was already friends, she sensed for the first time there was a barrier between her and Hogson which had never been there before.

She hoped that this was not a portent of the future, because she valued the friendships she had made with those who worked at Falcon and had no wish to lose them.

Somehow, with a charm and an instinct she felt she had learned from Chang, she managed to get back on the same easy footing they had been on before he began to think of her as his future mistress.

The same applied to the Housekeeper and the Curator.

The Butler was in her debt because she had brought him some special herbs for his rheumatism that her mother had distilled from an old recipe used by her famous grandmother.

At the same time, apart from the servants, the house itself seemed somehow different.

Now she found herself looking at it not only with admiration but knowing in the future it would be her home and she would belong there.

She could imagine nothing more wonderful than the joy of having all the books in the Library at her disposal, and being able to enjoy the pictures and the other treasures in the house whenever she wished.

At the same time they belonged to the man who would be her husband.

The more she thought about the Marquis, the more she realised that magnificent though he was, he was definitely a problem that she had to face, and it was not an easy one.

Finally she put her pride on one side and after a strenuous Karate lesson with Chang sat down cross-legged on the mattress and said:

"I want to talk to you!"

He sat as she did in the Yogi position, his back straight, his feet crossed under him. He too, of course, was now in the secret and looked at her with an understanding expression in his eyes.

Before she could speak he said:

"No need be worried, M'Lady. You think right, things come right! Everything falls in place!"

Elmina gave a little sigh.

"That sounds too easy, but of course I am worried. You know how overwhelming he is, Chang. Could he ever be interested in me as a person?"

It was a question which seemed to repeat itself over and over in her mind when she was alone at night.

She was intelligent enough to realise that as she had always taken third place to her beautiful sisters, Mirabel and Deirdre, she had very little confidence in herself as a woman.

She had grown up knowing that her birth had been a terrible disappointment to her father, and she was aware that as compensation, he treated her as if she were a boy.

He took her out riding with him, talked to her about the problems of running the Estate, and even allowed her to shoot beside him when he was alone, trying to make the best of a very bad job.

But he did not love her, and furthermore he did not admire her as he admired Mirabel.

He just put up with her because there was no alternative.

When Desmond was born and she saw the expression in her father's eyes when he looked at his son, it had hurt her almost unbearably.

She had wanted to beg him to love her just a little because he meant so much in her life.

Then she faced the unpalatable truth that no one, however willing, could turn on love like a tap, or for that matter, turn it off when it was no longer wanted.

She therefore tried to tell herself she was lucky to have had so much time with her father and there were still a few years left before Desmond would take her place and she would be completely unwanted.

Now, almost like a meteor streaking through the sky, the Marquis had suddenly appeared, and because neither Mirabel nor Deirdre wanted him, she was to bear his name and be his wife.

Yet her intelligence and all that Chang had taught her told her that it was not enough just to be the Marchioness of Falcon.

She wanted more, much more from the man she married.

She knew, to put it simply, that what she longed for and what she had never had was love.

When she thought about it she realised that she knew very little about love as between a man and a woman.

She had seen the way Robert looked at Mirabel, and how Christopher Bardsley's voice deepened when he spoke to Deirdre.

She was aware these were outward signs of something that they felt deeply within themselves, and what she supposed the novelists referred to as 'the passion of love.'

'Perhaps I shall never know that,' she thought wistfully.

On the evening that the Marquis was expected to dine with them, when she was dressed in her new gown, she stared at her reflection in the mirror.

The dressmakers had sent down from London three gowns which were each very different from the others.

One was of stiff white satin trimmed with pink roses, in which Mirabel would have looked like a goddess.

Elmina thought it took away the slimness of her figure and in some way did not enhance her skin or her hair.

It had always been a matter for conjecture as to why she had different coloured hair from her sisters.

Mirabel's was the gold of ripe corn, Deirdre's had the warmth of the sun late in the day, but Elmina's hair for some reason nobody could explain was so pale that her sisters had often said jokingly:

"If you had had pink eyes, you would have been an albino!"

At times it even seemed to have silver lights in it, and strangely even in the sunshine there was not that glint of red that appeared in Deirdre's, or the shine of gold in Mirabel's.

Because nobody appeared to take any interest in her appearance and, as Elmina told herself resignedly, the horses did not care, she had merely twisted the long strands of it, which reached to her waist, into a bun when she was riding.

At other times of the day she arranged it in a chignon then forgot about it.

Now she wondered if the Marquis would think it ugly, and her eyes as she looked at herself were extremely worried.

They too were not like her sisters' eyes, but seemed grey in some lights and in others had an undoubtedly green tint which made Deirdre say teasingly that they were cat's eyes and she must be able to see in the dark.

What was more surprising was the fact that she had eye-lashes which curved upwards like a child's and, while pale at the roots, darkened at the tips.

They made her eyes seem enormous because her face was by nature small and pointed.

Because of the amount of exercise she took, either riding every possible moment of the day or else battling energetically with Chang, there was not a superfluous ounce of flesh on her body.

In fact, she was too thin to be fashionable in the style set by the plump little Queen, who had grown progressively stouter every year since she married.

Although nobody at Warne Park was aware of it, Elmina had a unique beauty that was not as obvious as that of her sisters and had been hidden for years owing to the clothes she wore and her lack of interest in herself.

Now, because she was aware that her first meeting with the Marquis was an important one, she had taken a great deal of trouble.

While she had liked one of the other gowns that had come from London on approval, the one she decided to wear was the one her mother had said at first sight was quite unsuitable and should be sent back immediately.

It was made of a blue material shot with silver, and reminded Elmina of the darkening sky when the first stars brought a glimmer of light; interspersed amongst the blue were silver ribbons.

They caught the light every time she moved and seemed tonight, at any rate, to echo a touch of silver which appeared in her hair in the light from the candles.

The Queen had set the fashion for large skirts with a multitude of petticoats underneath them and a very small waist.

Above it the sloping shoulders were bare and a bertha fell gracefully over the bosom.

The bertha of Elmina's gown was embroidered with silver sequins to match the ribbons on the skirt and was transparent enough to reveal the curves of her breasts outlined by the blue material of the gown.

"I must say that looks better than I expected!" the Countess remarked. "But I think you would have been wiser to wear white."

"White does not suit me, Mama," Elmina said firmly, "but I like the other gown."

That was the soft pink of the musk roses that she had always loved in the garden.

But when she tried it on she thought it made her look almost too young to be married.

She had therefore decided to wear tonight the more sophisticated gown of blue and silver.

However, now, as she stared at her reflection in the mirror, she thought she did not look her eighteen years, which she had reached the previous week, but very much as she had done three or four years earlier.

But there was nothing she could do about it, and she was only sure, as she walked down the stairs, that the Marquis would compare her very unfavourably to the beautiful Lady Carstairs whom she was well aware was his fancy at the moment.

She had lingered so long in her bedroom that to her consternation she was only half-way down the stairs when she heard a carriage draw up outside the front door and realised the Marquis had arrived.

Barton was already at the top of the steps and two footmen had run a rather worn piece of red carpet, that had been used for some years, from the front door down to the carriage.

Elmina hesitated, not knowing whether to go down or return the way she had come, and, hesitating, was lost.

The Marquis, moving quickly as she might have expected, came in through the front door and while she was still indecisive he looked up and saw her.

There was therefore nothing she could do except walk on down the stairs towards him.

As she reached the hall he held out his hand.

"Good-evening!" he said as she curtsied. "I think you must be one of my host's daughters. I understand he has three."

"I am the youngest, My Lord."

"I am delighted to meet you," the Marquis said.

"My father and mother are waiting for you in the Drawing-Room," Elmina managed to say. "Will you come this way?"

The Marquis allowed his evening-cloak that was lined with red to be taken from his shoulders by Barton and handed a footman his high hat and gold-tipped cane.

Then he said to Elmina:

"I am ready!"

She was wondering frantically how she could tell him that she was his prospective bride.

Then she thought that it would be far too embarrassing and it would be better to leave it to her mother and father.

She was however vividly aware of how overpowering he seemed—much more so than when she had seen him from a distance in the Hunting-Field, or on the race-course.

She had also felt when his hand, from which he had now removed his gloves, touched hers that his vibrations were so strong that they seemed to prick her skin.

She had learnt from Chang that vibrations flowed not only from human beings but from everything that was alive.

He had told her how there were people in the world who drew strength and power from the trees, how the Buddhists would never pick a flower because they were destroying life and the Jains brushed the path in front of them when they walked for fear that they would kill an insect.

She knew that Chang's power over horses and, she was sure, over other animals arose from the vibrations he sent out towards them.

She tried to follow his lead and found she was gradually beginning to control her own vibrations so that she could use them deliberately rather than disperse them into the air without directing them to one particular point.

She wondered now if the Marquis felt that she vibrated to him as he did to her, but told herself it was extremely unlikely.

Barton had reached the door of the Drawing-Room, opened it with a flourish and announced in his usual stentorian tones:

"The Marquis of Falcon, M'Lady!"

Elmina paused to let the Marquis go ahead and she saw her family was grouped ready to greet their prestigious guest.

Her father was looking very distinguished in his evening-clothes, and her mother was glittering with diamonds.

Mirabel was looking lovely in the white gown in which she had been presented to the Queen.

Deirdre was wearing pale green, which Elmina knew was her favourite colour.

Quite suddenly all this pomp and ceremony for the sake of one man seemed to her amusing.

'We are all dressed up to kill,' she told herself, 'and there is really no reason for it, as the poor man is caught already, beyond any possibility of escape!'

She knew instinctively that, although the Marquis seemed genial enough, he was disliking the thought of matrimony and bored with having to go through the preliminaries of proposing to his future bride when the whole thing had been decided.

However she had to admit he was certainly making an effort, though she was sure her instinct was right and he found the whole thing incredibly tedious.

"Delightful to see you, Falcon," her father was saying, "and welcome!"

"Thank you," the Marquis replied. "It was very kind of you to invite me."

He kissed the Countess's hand and looked enquiringly at Mirabel, while Elmina, watching, knew he was thinking that she was exactly what he had expected.

The Marquis did in fact see a slight resemblance to Sapphire Carstairs and knew that Charles had been right in his description of her.

"May I present my eldest daughter, Mirabel?" the Earl said. "She is engaged, although it has not yet been announced, to Sir Robert Warrington, a neighbour whom I am sure you know."

With only the slightest pause of surprise the Marquis replied:

"Of course I know Robert, and I must congratulate him the next time we meet."

Mirabel curtsied gracefully and said:

"Thank you. Robert has often talked about you, My Lord, and how much he enjoys riding in your Steeple-Chases."

"And this is my second daughter, Deirdre," the Earl interrupted. "She is also engaged to be married, although it is a secret, to Christopher Bardsley. As I expect you are aware, his father, Lord Bardsley, is extremely ill and not expected to live."

It was obvious to Elmina that the Marquis was again somewhat taken aback.

But he merely wished Deirdre every happiness, and now there was a somewhat uncomfortable pause before the Earl said:

"I imagine you have already met my third daughter, Elmina, in the hall."

Now the Marquis turned to look at Elmina, who was standing a little behind him.

She was well aware there was an expression of astonishment in his eyes, which this time he could not conceal as he said as if he were at a loss for words:

"Yes—we met in the hall."

There was an awkward silence which was broken by Barton coming into the room followed by a footman carrying a silver tray on which there were glasses of champagne.

"I feel on this auspicious occasion," the Earl said, "that we should drink to it, and I hope you will enjoy this champagne, Falcon. It is a brand that was recommended to me years ago by King George, when he was on the throne."

"He was certainly reputed to be a great connoisseur of wine," the Marquis said conversationally.

There then began an exchange of reminiscences between the Earl and the Marquis of the parties they had attended in Royal Palaces.

"Alas, I was too young to know King George," the Marquis said, "but I always found the champagne offered at Windsor Castle by King William was undrinkable!"

"I agree with you," the Earl answered. "The poor man knew little about wine, and less about horses."

"There you are indeed right," the Marquis agreed. "You would be amazed at some of the animals that have been retained from his reign into this for no reason except that the Royal horses seem to linger on indefinitely. Nobody until now has ever turned them out to grass, even when they were too blind and too old to be of the least use."

"It is certainly a disgrace which only you are capable of putting right," the Earl said.

They talked of horses all through dinner, and although Elmina listened intently she made no attempt to join in the conversation.

Nor, as it happened, did either of her sisters, and although her mother occasionally made some remark, it became virtually a *tête-à-tête* between the Earl and the Marquis.

It was in fact a relief to the ladies when they could leave the gentlemen to their port.

As they reached the Drawing-Room Mirabel said:

"If that was not the most boring dinner I have ever attended, I cannot think of one to beat it!"

"Nor can I!" Deirdre said.

The two girls looked at Elmina and said:

"Dearest, we are so sorry for you."

"I was really quite interested," Elmina said, "but

70

I would have liked on one or two points to argue with His Lordship."

Mirabel gave a gasp.

"I am sure you should not do that! If you do, he might refuse to marry you!"

Elmina laughed.

"I doubt it. The reason why he is marrying is that he wanted to be appointed Master of the Horse, and he is enjoying every moment of that!"

"How do you know that, Elmina?" the Countess exclaimed. "I am sure your father did not tell you."

"Everybody has told me," Elmina replied, "because everybody knows it is the truth. In fact the Tinker, the Tailor, the Blacksmith, the Grooms, and even old Mrs. Blake in the village shop."

As she spoke she knew she had made a mistake, for her mother had no idea she had been to Falcon.

Mirabel noticed her slip and gave her a little frown, but fortunately the Countess was too concerned with her daughter's feelings to be aware of anything else.

"It would be a mistake, dearest," she said, "to believe everything you hear, and I am sure the Marquis, who I think is charming, had a very much more personal and important reason for being married than just because he wished to be Master of the Horse."

"But it certainly is the truth, Mama, and I can quite understand how much it means to him. After all, no one could be more capable of renovating the Royal Mews than he will be."

The Countess gave a little sigh, as if she did not wish to argue. Then she said:

"I am looking forward to seeing Falcon again. It is a long time since I last went there, but I hope, whatever it is like, you will be tactful, dear child, and not criticise in any way."

"No, of course not, Mama," Elmina agreed, and thought her mother looked relieved.

Because she was eager to be kind to her third daughter, the Countess went on.

"That is certainly a very becoming gown now you have it on, though I thought it looked quite different in the hand. I hope the day-gowns I ordered for you will be here tomorrow, but just in case His Lordship invited you somewhere in the daytime, it would be a mistake to buy too much before we go to London and see what is available."

"I agree with you, Mama," Elmina said, "and thank you very much for this gown. I like it!"

"It is certainly unusual," the Countess said. "At the same time I think you should have worn white. Mirabel looks far more like a future bride than you do!"

"I *am* a future bride, Mama!" Mirabel said.

She slipped her arm through Deirdre's and they moved to a corner of the room where they could talk privately to each other.

Elmina knew they were discussing the Marquis, and because she had sharp ears she heard Mirabel say:

"Having seen him at close-quarters, I only know that I love Robert a million times more than I did before!"

She heard her sisters laugh, and thinking that what

they were saying might upset her mother, she sat down on the sofa beside her.

"The Marquis is certainly very handsome, Mama," she said, "but I think he looks his best on a horse!"

"He has everything!" the Countess said as if she were following her own thoughts. "It is a pity that Mirabel . . ."

She stopped, knowing it would be unkind to her daughter to say what she was thinking, and Elmina said:

"It is too late for regrets, Mama. All I want you to do is to pray that I can make the Marquis the sort of wife he wants, and you know as well as I do that it will help Papa enormously to have him as a son-in-law."

The Countess looked startled.

There was no time for her to reply, for at that moment the Earl and the Marquis came into the Drawing-Room.

They walked across the room to where the Countess was sitting with Elmina, and the Earl said in a tone which told his daughter he thought it best to get on with it:

"The Marquis, my dear, is eager to see the pictures of your grandfather's horses by Stubbs in the Study, and I said you would show them to him."

"Yes, of course, Papa," Elmina agreed.

She was sure this had been planned by her father and mother before dinner, so she rose from the sofa and without looking at the Marquis led the way from the Drawing-Room.

They went along the passage to her father's Study where he had collected together all the best sporting pictures in the house.

The ones by Stubbs were certainly outstanding, and there was another by Sartorius which Elmina actually preferred.

She knew, however, this had been arranged to give the Marquis the opportunity of proposing to her, as he was expected to do, with a few well-chosen words.

She was not surprised when they reached the Study to find the candelabra were alight on the mantelpiece and on her father's desk.

She could not help, however, feeling a little nervous in case at the last moment the Marquis would feel he had been tricked into marrying her instead of Mirabel and now wished to back out of his proposition.

But he had evidently accepted the situation and knew that it did not make any difference to him, or in any case there was nothing he could do about it.

As they reached the center of the Study, which was quite a large room, he said as if he had rehearsed the speech to himself already:

"I think, Lady Elmina, you are aware that I have already asked your father if you will give me your hand in marriage. I hope the arrangement meets with your approval, and that I shall make you happy."

He spoke so formally that Elmina felt she would be expected to reply in the same vein. However she said, looking up at him:

"I should very much like to . . . marry you!"

"I am glad," the Marquis said. "I have brought

with me something which I hope you will like and will wear to show we are now officially engaged. A formal announcement of the fact will be in the *London Gazette* the day after tomorrow."

As he spoke he produced a jewel-box which he opened.

Inside was a magnificent oval-shaped diamond encircled by other diamonds.

Elmina looked at it, but did not speak and the Marquis said:

"This is the traditional engagement ring worn by all the Marchionesses of Falcon, but I will of course later give you a ring which will be your own and not part of the family collection."

"Thank you . . . very much," Elmina managed to say.

She put out her left hand and the Marquis put the ring on her third finger.

It was a little large and he said:

"I see it is rather big for you, and that of course can be adjusted later. But I thought you would like to have it tonight."

"It was . . . kind of you to . . . think of it."

She looked down at the ring and the Marquis, with a faint smile, as if he thought she was not being very enthusiastic, said:

"I should be interested to know what you are thinking."

To his surprise Elmina laughed. Then she said:

"You may think it ungrateful of me, but to be truthful I was thinking that this ring could buy a dozen of your wonderful horses!"

Now the Marquis was definitely surprised and he said:

"That is certainly something I did not expect you to say! I gather you are as fond of horses as your father is."

"Yes, indeed!" Elmina said. "I so much admire the horses I have seen you riding out hunting."

As she had already made one mistake, she realised she had to choose her words carefully, and the Marquis replied:

"You are making me feel uncomfortable, as I am not able to reply that I have noticed you."

"Why should you?" Elmina asked. "Actually, when one is hunting, I think it is wiser to concentrate on the fox rather than bother about the people who are watching!"

The Marquis laughed.

"That is true, but for most women it is a social gathering, which for them is the reason why they enjoy the meet."

"Not where I am concerned!" Elmina said. "I think that chitter-chatter is a terrible waste of time, and I know you feel the same."

She did not mention that the disdainful way in which he deliberately kept away from other members in the field had annoyed them and had made Mirabel describe him as being supercilious and behaving as if everybody else were his inferior.

"When we are married," the Marquis said, "I can promise you will be mounted on the best hunters I can provide for you."

He would have been very obtuse if he had not seen

the light that came into Elmina's eyes and the excitement that was in her voice as she said:

"I would rather have that than a million pounds' worth of diamonds!"

The Marquis laughed again.

"I think you will be able to have both!"

"Thank you, thank you very much indeed!" she said with an enthusiasm she had not shown when he had first given her the ring.

Then, as if she knew perceptively that he was considering whether or not it would be correct to kiss her, she said quickly:

"You had better admire Papa's pictures before we return to the Drawing-Room. He is very proud of them and would be very disappointed if you had not noticed them."

"I should have thought that in the circumstances he might have understood that I would be admiring you!" the Marquis said.

Elmina gave him what he thought was a mischievous look before she replied:

"That was very prettily spoken, and actually I hope it is the truth!"

"How could I do anything but protest that it is?" the Marquis asked with a faint note of amusement in his voice. "And will you forgive me if I ask what I suppose is a very impertinent question? How old are you?"

Elmina laughed, and although she was not aware of it, it was a very musical sound.

"I was certain that was what you were wondering when you first looked at me," she said. "I was, as it happens, eighteen last week. I know I look younger but, although it may trouble you, I can assure you it is something which will be remedied as the years go by."

Now the Marquis also laughed quite genuinely as he said:

"That is indisputable. At the same time, I admit I was not expecting anyone who looked so young and, if you will forgive me for saying so, so unusual."

"You did say in your letter to Papa that you wished to marry his daughter! As I am the only one available, you really did not have much choice."

"I am not complaining," the Marquis said quickly.

He had the strange feeling as he spoke that Elmina did not believe him.

Then she said, which surprised him even more than anything else that had happened that evening:

"I think now we should return to the Drawing-Room. Mama would be very shocked if we stayed here too long, and Papa will be apprehensive in case having seen me you want to change your mind and look around for a bride elsewhere."

The Marquis was so astonished that for a moment he was speechless and could only stare at her.

Then, as she had already reached the door and opened it, he found there was nothing he could do but follow her from the room.

Only when they were outside in the corridor and walking back the way they had come did he say:

"I was certainly right, Lady Elmina, in thinking that you were unusual, and I look forward to our next meeting."

"That is in three days' time, when we are coming to dine with you, My Lord," Elmina replied. "And of course I am greatly looking forward to seeing Falcon and all its treasures, even though at that time of the evening I shall not be able to meet your horses."

He thought he should make some reply, but as Elmina, walking ahead of him, opened the door into the Drawing-Room, the Marquis had a strange feeling that while she was speaking there was beneath the quite common-place words some joke that she was keeping to herself.

He did not understand why he felt this. It just came into his mind and he felt sure he was not mistaken.

All he could think about as an hour later he drove back alone to his own house was that his future bride did not look as he had expected, nor did she say what he might have expected her to say.

Instead he could only sum her up in one word: 'Unusual.'

chapter four

ELMINA went slowly down the stairs to where her
father, who like the rest of her family seemed con-
siderably agitated, was waiting for her in the hall.

He drew his gold watch out of his waist-coat pocket
as she appeared and said:

"Come on, come on! You are late!"

It was impossible for Elmina to move quickly with
the long veil being carried by her mother's lady's-
maid.

Because she was afraid of tripping she was holding
on to the banisters.

Her father did not watch her descend, for which
she was grateful, for she was already anticipating a
somewhat hostile reaction to her wedding-gown.

After they had dined at Falcon, where the dinner-
party had been different from when the Earl dined at

Warne Park because he had invited some of his relatives to join them, she had had no chance to talk to him alone, nor had he made any effort to single her out.

She knew that while his marriage had the approval of his relations, they were undoubtedly surprised at his choice.

Every one of them remarked upon how young she looked, and few were able to believe that she was actually eighteen.

She knew too that they had expected Mirabel to be the daughter chosen by the Marquis, and a number of people had therefore to be taken into the secret of her engagement.

On one thing Elmina was determined, which was that she would look her very best on her wedding-day, being aware there would be a great number of the Marquis's friends coming from London to look with curiosity at the bride, and undoubtedly criticise.

She was fortunate that the Countess was so agitated at the idea of having three weddings in so short a time that she did not concentrate as much on Elmina's as she might otherwise have done.

When they went to London she took her youngest daughter to the shops she always patronised herself, chose a number of gowns that she thought suitable, and said she would like to see sketches and patterns the following day.

It was an opportunity for Elmina to suggest that since her mother had a number of other things to do in London and a great many invitations from friends, she and Mirabel should go back together to the shops accompanied by a lady's-maid.

The Countess was relieved and so was Mirabel.

"You know what Mama is like," she said to her sister. "She always thinks she knows better than we do, and quite frankly I want to please Robert, who has very definite ideas about what I should wear."

Elmina did not say anything, but she thought the same thing applied to the Marquis, and she had no intention of being a rather dull, conventional bride in white satin.

This, of course, was what her mother had chosen, and therefore when she went back to the shop the next day she countermanded the order and chose instead a soft gauze embroidered all over with silver.

It was lovely and expensive, but Elmina knew it would become her and would certainly accentuate the lights in her hair and the clarity of her skin.

Because she had never been allowed to have any clothes of her own and nobody had troubled until now what she looked like, she had often lain awake at night designing herself fairy clothes.

She thought they would change her from being an insignificant youngest sister, small and unwanted, into a Princess who would of course capture the vacillating heart of Prince Charming.

Generally she saw herself in her fantasies wearing a breath-takingly beautiful riding-habit and mounted on a black stallion that could out-ride and out-jump every horse in England.

Alternatively, she appeared at the Ball later than

any of the other guests and was dressed either in a gown covered with diamonds that glittered like stars, or in one that resembled the moonlight.

The latter had to be her choice as a bride, and the gauze, certainly at a distance, gave the impression that she had stepped out of a woodland stream.

The dressmaker her mother patronised had an artistic soul, so she well understood what Elmina wanted besides being impressed by the fact that she was to be the Marchioness of Falcon.

She therefore agreed to keep her choice a secret from the Countess and to ensure that her gown looked different from that of any other bride who had been married since Queen Victoria came to the throne.

"You look lovely, M'Lady!" she said at the last fitting, and there was no doubt that she was speaking sincerely.

"Thank you," Elmina replied. "I do hope you are right."

Even as she spoke she knew that what she really was hoping was that the Marquis would admire her.

At the same time she could not be confident that he would even notice what she was wearing when undoubtedly Lady Carstairs would be in the congregation.

He had, however, taken the trouble to send to Warne Park a selection of diamond tiaras, saving the Countess's face by saying it was traditional for the Falcon brides to wear the family jewels on their wedding-day.

The Countess genuinely believed this, but Elmina suspected that the Marquis was thinking everything they possessed was very inferior to what he owned.

Also she was sure that he wanted to organise as much as possible himself because he could trust nobody else to do it so competently.

After they had arranged the day of the wedding he had said casually but in a manner which told Elmina he had already thought it out:

"I think, My Lord, it would be far easier if the Reception could be at Falcon, rather than in your house."

The Earl had looked surprised and the Marquis had gone on.

"As you are well aware, I shall have to provide marquees in which my tenants and employees can have the wedding-feast they expect, and of course there will be fireworks in the evening."

He paused to go on slowly.

"It seems somewhat laborious for Elmina and me to have to rush from the Reception here back to Falcon in time for me to make a speech in both marquees, and of course introduce my wife."

The way he put it seemed so reasonable that the Earl had agreed without much show of reluctance.

The Earl was also thinking that it would save him a great deal of expense, and he was already counting the cost of Mirabel's Reception and later Deirdre's.

It was therefore agreed that they should be married in the little Church where Elmina had been christened and where all her ancestors were buried.

They would go from there straight to Falcon, where the Reception would be held in the huge Ball-Room.

She learnt that the Marquis had arranged that at

the point where they would receive their guests they would have a background of orchids grown in his own greenhouses.

The whole Ball-Room was to be decorated by his gardeners in a spectacular fashion which her father could not even have begun to emulate.

In fact, when Mirabel and Deirdre spent the day before the wedding decorating the little Church just inside the Park, they were quite certain that the lilies and carnations would look very meagre in comparison with the Marquis's idea of decoration.

This made Elmina more determined than ever not to look a small, insignificant country daisy.

She was quite certain, anyway, that Lady Carstairs would be an exotic orchid with whom she could not begin to compete.

She therefore had to concentrate all her imaginings on herself, and it was something she had very seldom done in the past.

It was a subject on which she could not appeal to Chang, and yet she felt that in a way he helped her because he had taught her to look inward for what she wanted and find the answer within herself.

When she was alone she practised breathing deeply in the manner the monks had taught their pupils to do before they could learn Karate.

Almost at once she saw in her mind a picture, and then it was easy to order what she wanted, and to know that whatever anybody else might say she would do what she wished to do.

Her mother had produced with pride the Brussels

lace veil that had been in the Warne family for two hundred years.

Elmina knew that on Mirabel it would look beautiful, but it was too heavy for her, and since there was a silver pattern on the gauze gown it was a mistake for her to have a patterned veil as well.

The dressmaker had produced a tulle that was not white but the shade of a morning mist, and had sewn on it tiny specks of diamanté which glittered in the light and looked like drops of dew.

Again choosing to defy tradition, Elmina refused to have a train and instead suggested that the sparkling tulle should trail behind her up the aisle.

The next difficulty was the tiaras.

The Marquis had sent three of them, each one larger than the next, and all of them overwhelming on herself.

"They are glorious! Absolutely glorious!" Mirabel cried.

She put one on her head and said:

"Promise me, when I am married you will let me borrow this one. It is quite the most impressive crown I shall ever have the chance of wearing."

"Of course you can borrow it!" Elmina replied.

At the same time she knew it was wrong for her.

She looked despairingly at the other two tiaras. Then when she was still wondering what she should do her father said to her:

"It seems ridiculous for me to spend a lot of money I have not got, on giving you an expensive wedding-present, when your future husband is so rich."

"You must not be extravagant, Papa," Elmina replied.

"At the same time," the Earl ruminated, "people will think it very strange if I do not give you a piece of jewellery of some sort."

"There is no need..." she began.

"What I thought," the Earl continued as if she had not spoken, "is you can have the wreath of wild flowers which your grandmother wore when she was quite a young girl."

Elmina gave a little gasp, knowing it was something she had always admired and loved, but which had been kept in the safe and she had never seen it worn.

The Countess had a much more impressive tiara that she preferred, and her father had always said that as the wreath was so old the stones might be loose and he had no wish to risk losing one.

Now when he had it cleaned Elmina knew it was exactly what she needed as a bride.

It was a circle of wild flowers skillfully worked by one of the great jewellers of the eighteenth century, and there was a portrait of her grandmother wearing it when she was twelve years old.

"You could not give me anything I would like better, Papa," Elmina cried, "and thank you very, very much!"

The Earl was rather surprised at her enthusiasm and arranged to send it with all the other presents she had received to Falcon, where they would be on show during the Reception.

Elmina however had managed to extract it from its velvet-lined box before it actually left the house.

She was therefore able to put it on her head over the veil without anybody being aware that she was not going to appear in the Church in one of the Falcon tiaras.

There had been another struggle over her bouquet.

Her mother insisted that she should have one of white carnations and lilies, which the gardeners were expected to make for her.

But while the Marquis was still in London Elmina had ridden over to Falcon without anybody being aware of where she was going.

She left her horse in the stables with Hogson, who was delighted to see her.

"We was thinking as 'ow you'd forgotten us, M'Lady!" he said.

"You will not be saying that when you see me every day!" Elmina smiled. "Then perhaps you will have too much of me!"

"That'd be impossible, M'Lady!" Hogson said, "an' there's several new 'orses to show ye, which I'm sure you'll think better than anything we've had before."

"That would be impossible!"

As she spoke she went into the stalls to meet the newcomers and went over their points with Hogson, one by one.

Then she told him she had to go to the gardens and went off to find the Head Gardener.

He too was a man she knew well from past visits, and he supposed she had come to see how the orchids with which he was intending to decorate the Ball-Room were progressing.

"They'll be in flower at exactly the right moment, M'Lady!" he said proudly.

"How would they dare do anything else!" Elmina smiled.

Then she said:

"I need your advice, and it is very important."

Lester, for that was his name, listened attentively as she explained to him that her bridal gown was different from anybody else's and it would completely ruin the effect if she had to carry the traditional bouquet of carnations and lilies.

Lester was one of the leading gardeners in the country, and the Marquis had in fact persuaded him to leave Kew Gardens to come and fill his own greenhouses with exotic flowers.

He understood exactly what Elmina wanted, and found her what was an orchid, but a very strange one.

Its petals, although white, had an almost translucent look about them and were faintly speckled with green that might have resembled the sunshine on a clear stream.

As soon as she saw them Elmina realised that they were exactly what she had seen in the picture she had looked inwards to see, and that the orchids in some way resembled her eyes.

"We've got just enough of them, M'Lady, for a small bouquet," Lester said, "and if you're carrying them, it'll be a surprise to His Lordship, because this is the first year they've bloomed."

Elmina drew in her breath.

"You must not tell him I am having them," she said, "in case he prevents me from doing so."

The Head Gardener laughed.

"It'll be a secret between you an' me, M'Lady, but I can't believe he'd be angry. Even if he is, it'll be too late for him to do anything about it!"

"That is what I thought!" Elmina said.

Her bouquet had been delivered to Warne Park just a few minutes before she came downstairs.

She had made it clear that it had to arrive after her mother had left for the Church, and it was there waiting for her now on a settle in the hall beside the white bouquet provided by their own gardeners.

She moved across to the one she intended to carry and as she picked it up she had an idea.

"Put the white bouquet in the carriage," she said to one of the footmen.

As he did so the Earl was aware of what was happening.

"What do you want two bouquets for?" he asked suspiciously.

"I thought it would be nice, Papa, to put the white one on Grandmama's grave, which is just inside the lych-gate."

The Earl looked surprised, then he said:

"What do you want to do that for?"

"I have been thinking of Grandmama today and how everybody admired her, and, as you see, I am wearing the wreath of flowers that once belonged to her, and which you have now given to me."

The Earl looked even more surprised. At the same time he was more concerned with getting Elmina to the Church.

"All right then, come along!" he said. "We cannot stay here talking and it will doubtless annoy Falcon if we keep him waiting."

Elmina's eyes twinkled.

"I think it would be a new experience for him."

Her father was however not listening.

Elmina had her own way and as she walked towards the Church porch her father handed her the white bouquet and she laid it on her grandmother's grave.

As she did so she said a little prayer.

"You were so successful, Grandmama, that nobody has ever forgotten you," she said. "I think too that Grandpapa loved you until he died. Help me to be like you."

Then as the onlookers from the village wished her good-luck and murmured amongst themselves at her appearance, Elmina holding on to her father's arm walked into the crowded Church where the Marquis was waiting for her.

* * *

Driving swiftly from the village towards Falcon in a well-sprung carriage drawn by four perfectly matched horses, their harness decorated with flowers, Elmina thought this was the first time she had been alone with her husband.

This however was not the moment to have an intimate conversation with him.

Because it was a warm, sunny day, the Marquis had the hood of the carriage open, and that also was decorated with flowers.

All the way to Falcon as they passed through the small villages first on the Earl's estate, and then on the Marquis's, the villagers crowded to see them go by.

Many of the children threw small bunches of flowers into the open carriage or else pelted them with roses and rose-petals.

Elmina and the Marquis were concerned with waving their acknowledgements and he ordered his coachman to go more slowly so that the villagers got a chance to see them.

Only as they drove in through the impressive gates of Falcon did the Marquis say in what Elmina felt was a bored voice:

"Now we really have to face the music! The majority of my friends from London did not bother to come to the Church and my secretary anticipates that we shall have to shake nearly a thousand hands before we are finished!"

"It would be much easier if we were like the Chinese and bowed politely," Elmina said. "I sympathise most sincerely with their desire not to be touched."

She spoke without thinking and she thought the Marquis gave her a sharp glance before he said:

"I suppose it is one of the penalties of getting married, and we cannot grumble, as it happens only once in a lifetime."

"That is certainly a consoling thought," Elmina replied.

Then she gave a little cry of excitement, for as they progressed down the drive she could see ahead of them two large marquees erected on the lawn.

They were decorated with flowers and flags that were waving in the breeze and looked extremely pretty against the huge grey stone house with the Marquis's standard flying on the roof.

The tenants and employees of the two estates were however not inside the marquees, but were making a large crowd outside the entrance with its long flight of steps, where the Marquis and Elmina would alight.

They cheered heartily as they did so, the men waving their hats in the air, the women their handkerchiefs.

When they reached the top of the steps, bride and bridegroom stood waving in reply.

"We will be able to talk to them later," the Marquis said, and while the cheers were still ringing out they walked into the hall.

Elmina had seen it so often before that she had ceased to be surprised by its fine proportions.

There were exquisitely sculpted statues of gods and goddesses in niches round the walls, and the ebony and crystal staircase curved up on one side to the State Rooms on the First Floor.

They were however to proceed directly to the Ball-Room and that involved walking for some distance down the wide corridors ornamented with antique furniture and some very valuable pictures.

It would have been impossible for Elmina to move over the carpets for such a long way without somebody carrying her veil.

A footman was designated to do so, and she was able to walk at quite a good pace beside the Marquis.

He did not offer her his arm and she felt he was scowling, as if he were not looking forward to the crowd which was waiting for them.

Her veil had been lifted back from her face in the Vestry when they had signed the Marriage Register, and now she had a quick glance at herself in the mirrors as they passed them.

She saw that the softness of the tulle with the diamonds in her grandmother's wreath gleaming through it looked more becoming than anything else she had ever worn.

At the same time she could not help feeling that the Marquis would have preferred to have married Mirabel, who because Robert was present in the congregation had looked more beautiful than ever, and in Elmina's eyes was not really eclipsed by Lady Carstairs.

Elmina had expected that like most of the Marquis's other friends she would go directly to Falcon.

But she had seen her in the third pew on the Marquis's side of the Church when she came up the aisle on her father's arm and knew that it would be impossible for anybody to look more lovely.

Wearing blue, the colour of her eyes, with a bonnet covered in feathers of the same colour and with a profusion of turquoises and diamonds, she stood out in the Church which, Elmina thought, she had obviously intended to do.

Now as she and the Marquis took their places beside her father and mother and everybody began to surge forward to shake their hands, she saw that Lady Carstairs was one of the first.

Having barely touched the Earl's and Countess's hands with the tips of her fingers, she then clasped the Marquis's in both of hers as she said in a soft voice that sounded like the purring of a cat:

"You know that I pray, Alston dear, for your happiness."

Her blue eyes looked up into his, and Elmina thought for one startled moment that she intended to kiss him.

Then she turned away and in a voice that was palpably insincere said to Elmina:

"I am so delighted to meet you, and because your husband is such a very old friend of mine, I hope we shall be friends too."

It certainly sounded very pleasant, but Elmina knew with the perception Chang had taught her that the beautiful Lady Carstairs was her enemy and always would be.

Then, like the advancing waves of the sea, people came up to them, shook hands, wished them happiness, and walked on.

It went on and on until there appeared to be no more, and at last the queues had vanished and their guests were all drinking champagne and eating the delicacies which the Chefs at Falcon had been cooking for days.

"Now we cut the cake!" the Marquis said briskly, almost as if he thought they were running behind schedule.

He walked to where it towered four tiers high, and

decorated with the traditional horse-shoes, white heather, silver bells and orange-blossom.

The only innovation was that instead of two dolls dressed as the bride and groom on top there was a replica of one of the Marquis's horses wearing his colours.

Elmina had already been told what had been planned, and as she looked up at it she said:

"What could be more appropriate? And of course an omen that you will win even more races this year than you did last, if that is possible!"

The Marquis smiled.

Then somebody produced his sword and they cut the cake together and at last were able to move amongst the guests.

Then the Marquis said:

"I want you, Elmina, to meet one of my oldest and most important friends: Major Charles Marriott!"

Elmina glanced at the good-looking young man smiling at her and told herself she liked him.

"I am delighted to meet you!" he said as the Marquis moved off to speak to somebody else. "I feel I ought to congratulate Alston on finding a bride who is so original."

"If you mean my gown," Elmina said, "I am sure most people will find something derogatory to say about it."

"I am quite certain they will not do that," Charles Marriott replied. "You look like a water-Siren—if that is the right description!"

"That is just what I had hoped to look like."

"But actually," Charles Marriott went on, "it is not only your gown, but you, who are not at all what I expected."

Elmina laughed.

"That is because you were thinking of my sister. But she is already engaged, and I was the only one who was eligible for the post."

"I am certainly not complaining," Charles Marriott replied, "and I am sure Alston is not either. It is only right that being so unusual himself he should have a bride who is different."

As he spoke they both looked, as if drawn by a magnet, to the Marquis and saw he was talking to Lady Carstairs, who was staring up at him with an expression on her face which even the most casual onlooker would have thought indiscreet.

Charles Marriott looked back at Elmina.

"You are unusual in yourself," he said, "and no woman really wants to be a reflection of somebody else."

Elmina knew exactly what he was saying to her and she said:

"Thank you. I was feeling a little frightened that I had done the wrong thing, but now you have reassured me."

"I promise you I mean it," Charles Marriott said, "and you must be aware that you look very, very beautiful!"

He saw the surprise in her eyes, then as the colour came into her face at his compliment he told himself that not only was she unusual but with his unfailing good-luck Alston, when he least expected it, had achieved another win.

Charles Marriott had no chance for another word with Elmina, for before she had talked to half-a-dozen people, the Marquis came to her side to tell her it was time they went to the marquees to welcome and meet their other guests.

By the time he had made two speeches, and the bride and bridegroom had been toasted with beer and home-brewed cider, it was time for the majority of their guests to leave.

Once again it was the Marquis who had decided that the first part of their honeymoon should be spent at Falcon.

Her father and mother had thought it strange, but Elmina guessed it was because he thought it would be boring to be alone with his wife in one of his other houses where he did not have so much to do as at Falcon.

His excuse was that he not only had a number of his own horses to see to which had only just arrived, but also there was a local Sale he wished to attend in order to purchase horses for the Royal Mews.

They could therefore decide a week or so later if they wished to go elsewhere.

Elmina, as it happened, was very content to stay at Falcon.

She knew the horses there would be better than they would be anywhere else and she was looking forward also to finding time for browsing in the Library.

She was already aware that it contained a large number of books on subjects which she and Chang had often discussed and in which they were particularly interested.

A week or so before the wedding she had said to him:

"You must not think, Chang, because I will be married, that I wish to give up my Karate or Ju Jitsu. As soon as I can arrange it, I want you to come over to Falcon, or else I will come here for a lesson. It would be a mistake to get out of practice."

"May be difficult, M'Lady," Chang said.

"Nothing is too difficult if we make up our minds to do it," Elmina replied. "That is what you taught me, and you cannot argue about it now."

"That's true, M'Lady." Chang grinned. "If one wants anything enough then it becomes ours."

"That is what I want to believe," Elmina said in a low voice, "and I know that when I practise with you it has taught me to think more clearly and concentrate more directly."

"That is what Karate means," Chang agreed.

"I will work out something," Elmina said.

She was actually thinking that the Marquis would have a great many interests in which he would not allow her to take part, and when she was free she could be with Chang and he could go on teaching her as he had already.

Finally the last guest had left and although there were a number of people still in the marquees, inside the great house all was quiet.

The Marquis looked at his watch.

"We will have dinner in an hour," he said, "and I expect you would like a bath. I know I want one."

"I feel rather as if I have had a very hard day's hunting," Elmina said, "and there is still a long ride home."

The Marquis gave one of his short, sharp laughs that she had decided meant he was slightly amused but not enough to laugh heartily.

She picked up her veil and folded it over one arm, then turned towards the door and the Marquis said:

"I feel I should have congratulated you on your gown, but I was rather disappointed you did not wear one of my tiaras."

"They made me look top-heavy!" Elmina explained. "And they would, I thought, attract too much attention."

The Marquis raised his eye-brows.

"That is what most women want."

Elmina's eyes twinkled.

"I thought it was a question of either diamonds or me," she said, "and today, at any rate, I wanted it to be me!"

Now the Marquis did laugh as he said:

"That is certainly a different way of looking at it, and you, Elmina, are decidedly different!"

"Thank you," she said, "and I suppose I should thank you for my bouquet."

"I could not believe there was anybody else in the country who could have provided you with those particular orchids."

"As they were exactly what I wanted, I hope you will not grudge them to me."

"How could I?" he enquired lightly. "Actually Charles told me that they matched your eyes."

"I like your friend Charles," Elmina said, "and that was what I thought myself, although I was too modest to say so!"

She started up the stairs before the Marquis could say any more and when she reached the bedroom she knew, because she had seen it before. It was where all the Marchionesses of Falcon had slept.

She wondered if the Marquis had realised she had found her way without either his escorting her, or sending for the Housekeeper to do so.

Mrs. Leonard was waiting for her in the State Bed-room.

"You look lovely, M'Lady, you do really!" she exclaimed. "A real picture, although some of them were surprised you were not wearing white."

"The answer to that is that I do not look my best in white," Elmina replied.

"Well, all I can say, M'Lady, is that most of the unmarried women among your guests are now saving up to afford silver for their own weddings, but they haven't got hair like you, M'Lady, unless they get it out of a dye-bottle."

After Elmina had had a bath in what had originally been a Powder-Closet opening out of the State Bed-room, she put on a pink gown that she had bought in London.

It was a very soft pink, but was not the same as

the musk-rose gown, which had made her look so young.

It was ornamented with camelias in the same colour, which were arranged low on the shoulders from which there hung a bertha.

It was a lovely and very elaborate gown. At the same time Elmina thought when she looked in the mirror that she appeared as if she were still in the School-Room, and merely dressed up for the occasion.

"There is nothing I can do about it," she told her reflection, "and he will just have to take me as I am."

They had dinner not in the huge Baronial Hall in which they had dined when she had come to dinner at Falcon with her parents.

Instead it was in a small Dining-Room decorated by Robert Adam with his soft green, and lit only by the candles on a small and intimate table.

It had an atmosphere, Elmina thought, that was conducive to two people who should be talking of love.

But they talked of horses, and the Marquis told Elmina how much he was looking forward to showing her the following day the new horses he had recently bought.

She did not tell him she had seen them already and thought them superb, but merely listened attentively to what he had to say.

She thought that actually she had never enjoyed a meal so much, or been with a man who was so interesting and knowledgeable on his own subject.

As they dined late, it was eleven o'clock before they moved into one of the small Salons which had been decorated with white flowers and looked very bridal.

"If you do not think it rude of me," Elmina said, "I would like now to go to bed. It has been a long day, and as I know you like riding before breakfast, I would not want to keep you waiting."

"I would like to leave at about seven-thirty," the Marquis said, "but if you are tired, you must say so."

"I shall certainly not feel too tired to ride any horse that belongs to you," Elmina answered. "So, goodnight, My Lord. I promise I will not keep you waiting."

She did not wait for his reply but hurried upstairs, where one of the younger maids was waiting to help her with her gown.

Mrs. Leonard had already told her that she would be provided with her own personal lady's-maid as soon as she could interview some.

Elmina was so used to looking after herself and helping her sisters that she could not really imagine what a personal maid would find to do all the time.

However it was nice to have everything ready for her, and she put on one of the pretty diaphanous nightgowns that had been in her trousseau, then over it a summer wrap, almost as light, trimmed with lace and ornamented with little bows of blue velvet ribbon.

"Do not wait," she said to the maid as the young woman stood irresolute.

The maid, having bobbed a curtsy, went from the room.

Elmina having blown out the candles except for

those beside the bed, went behind the curtains to stand at an open window looking out onto the garden in the moonlight.

She wanted to think and remember what had happened to her, and how although it still seemed like one of the stories she made up for herself, she was now the wife of the Marquis of Falcon.

She was mistress of this exquisite house and could share with her husband the horses in the stables and all his other possessions, including the huge Library waiting for her downstairs.

"I cannot believe it!" she said. "It cannot be true!"

She sent a little prayer winging into the moonlight that she would not be crushed or overwhelmed either by the Marquis or his possessions but might, although it would be difficult, eventually make him aware of her as a woman.

After she had stood for what seemed quite a long time she told herself she must go to bed.

Tomorrow would be another exciting day and she had no wish to be tired.

As she came back into the room, pulling the curtains to behind her, the door opened into what she knew was the communicating room where the Marquis slept, and he came in.

He was wearing a crimson velvet robe which Elmina thought made him look just as impressive as when he was in the clothes he wore in the daytime.

She had wondered if he would seem different if she saw him without either the magnificence of his evening-dress or the elegance of his riding-breeches and boots.

Now with the frills round his silk night-shirt high against his neck almost like a cravat, and the red of his robe accentuated by the darkness of his hair, he looked, she thought, almost as if he had stepped out of a picture.

He glanced first towards the empty bed and now he looked at her with a slight air of surprise as she came from behind the curtains.

"Not in bed, Elmina?" he asked. "I thought you were tired!"

"I was just looking at the moon."

Then as she moved a few steps towards him she stopped and asked:

"Why are you here?"

"Why am I here?" he repeated. "I think the answer to that is very obvious. You are my wife!"

She was very still before she said:

"You do not mean . . . you cannot think . . ."

She hesitated and the Marquis looked at her in surprise before he said:

"You were not expecting me?"

"No . . . of course not! And I cannot believe you are . . . thinking . . . of . . ."

She was feeling for words and the Marquis said:

"I know this has all been done in rather a hurry, and we have not had time to get to know each other well. At the same time, Elmina, you are my wife and I am looking forward to making our marriage a very happy one."

"I . . . I think I understand what you are . . . saying," she said, "but I . . . never imagined for one . . . moment that you would expect . . . me to behave like your wife . . . before we have even talked about it or . . . had a chance to . . . get to know each other."

She found it difficult to say what was in her mind and the Marquis said with a faint smile:

"We have to start somewhere, and what could be better than to start on our wedding-night?"

"That is . . . impossible."

"What do you mean—impossible?"

"Because it would . . . spoil everything from the . . . very beginning."

"I do not understand."

She was hesitating how to tell him what was in her mind and he said:

"I think quite frankly it would be a mistake to get involved in words when there is a very much easier way for us to get to know each other, and a very much more natural one."

He walked towards Elmina as he spoke and she knew by the expression on his face he was going to put his arms around her and kiss her.

Instinctively she put up her hands to prevent him, and stepping backwards said:

"No, no! It is too soon, much too soon . . . and I cannot let you . . . touch me!"

"*You* cannot let me?" the Marquis repeated. "I doubt if you would be able to prevent it, and quite frankly, Elmina, you must allow me to know what is best for both of us in this."

"No!" Elmina said. "No . . . please . . . I want to . . . talk to you!"

"There is nothing to talk about," the Marquis replied. "I think you have forgotten that you promised

107

in the Marriage Service to obey me, and that is now what I expect you to do!"

He moved towards her again.

Then, as he put out his hands to take hold of her, Elmina reacted instinctively without really thinking about it.

One moment the Marquis was on his feet, pulling her firmly and determinedly into his arms.

The next, to his complete and utter astonishment, he found himself staggering backwards from a blow from something hard and strong which struck him in his solar plexus, and against which he had no defence whatsoever.

Then he was sitting on the floor looking up at his wife with an almost ludicrous expression of surprise on his handsome face.

chapter five

FOR a moment there was silence, then Elmina faltered:

"I ... I am sorry ... I am so ... sorry."

"How the devil did you do that?" the Marquis enquired.

He did not rise, but only sat looking at her as if he could not believe it had really happened.

"I ... I am ... sorry," she said again. "Please ... do not be angry."

"I think I am more surprised than angry ..." he began.

Then, looking at her standing in front of him in her diaphanous night-clothes, he suddenly began to laugh.

"This cannot be true!" he said. "It is impossible!"

Then as she still stood there irresolute, not knowing what to do, he said:

"If you want to talk to me, and I realise it is something we must do, get into bed."

As she hesitated he added:

"If it will make you happy, I promise not to touch you."

There was a note of sarcasm in his voice which Elmina did not perceive because she was so perturbed at what she had done.

Actually the Marquis, as he got slowly to his feet, was thinking that, while he had known already that his wife was unusual, this was the most extraordinary thing that had ever happened in the whole of his life.

By the time he was standing up Elmina had slipped between the lace-edged sheets.

It was a very magnificent bed with a canopy of carved gold angels, the posts also gilded with hangings of beautifully embroidered *eau-de-nile* velvet which had mellowed with age.

Against the pillows Elmina looked very small and insubstantial, and with her fair hair falling over her shoulders it was difficult to think she was anything but a child.

The Marquis however was aware, as she was not, of the transparency of her nightgown which revealed the curves of her breasts, and her large eyes looking up at him apprehensively were those of a woman.

He sat down a little gingerly on the side of the mattress facing her and said:

"Now, let us start again. Tell me first how you knocked me down in that extraordinary manner."

"It was . . . Karate."

"Karate?" the Marquis ejaculated. "How in God's name can you know Karate?"

Elmina drew in her breath.

"I have been...practising it and Ju Jitsu for... over a year."

"But how? And where? I cannot imagine there are many experts in that unusual science in Oxfordshire."

Elmina gave him a little smile.

"The explanation is that Chang, one of my father's servants, is a master at both Arts."

"He obviously has a very proficient pupil," the Marquis said somewhat dryly.

He rubbed the front of his body as he spoke and Elmina asked quickly:

"I...I did not really...hurt you?"

He shook his head. Then he said:

"Now that you have demonstrated very forcibly that you do not wish to be touched, I am prepared to listen to your arguments as to why we should not lead a normal life as man and wife."

Elmina looked embarrassed and turned her head away to look across the room.

He knew that she was wondering what she should say.

"I want the truth, Elmina," he said firmly, "and if you think it is a mistake for me to do what I intended, I would like to hear from you a reasonable argument against it."

"My first reason is...very simple," Elmina said in a very low voice. "You are...in love with the beautiful Lady Carstairs!"

111

The Marquis stiffened.

"How can you possibly know anything about Lady Carstairs?"

The enquiry was so unexpected that Elmina turned her head to look at him, her eyes wide, the light from the candles glinting in them and making them seem very green.

"Everybody knows you are . . . enamoured of her."

"What do you mean—everybody?"

She made a very expressive gesture with her hands and as she did not speak, the Marquis went on.

"It is unthinkable that you should know anything about the lady in question, unless, of course, you have listened to the gossip in London."

"I did not see anybody when I was in London buying my trousseau," Elmina answered. "But long before you asked Papa if you could marry me, everybody round here, in our house, yours, and in the villages was talking about Her Ladyship and how beautiful she is."

"Are you really telling me the truth?" the Marquis asked.

For the first time since she had knocked him down Elmina smiled as she said:

"Surely you know everybody in the neighbourhood talks about you? You are the most exciting, besides being the most magnificent person they have ever seen! So naturally everything you do and every lady you love is of absorbing interest to the oldest inhabitants in the cottages no less than to those who live in the big houses."

"I can hardly believe it!" the Marquis ejaculated.

"Are you not being very modest about yourself? After all, there have been a great many beautiful ladies, one after another, to keep us all interested."

"I cannot imagine why your father and mother allowed you to listen to such gossip!" the Marquis said crossly.

"Papa and Mama talk about you too, of course they do, and you can hardly expect them to respect your good name, if that is what you are worrying about, considering you have never invited them to Falcon!"

Again the Marquis stared at her.

"You mean—they expected to be invited?"

Elmina's laughter rang out and it was a very attractive sound.

"Everyone who was not invited, and that included all your neighbours, was very disappointed. They heard about your parties and waited expectantly for an invitation which never came."

"I had no idea!" the Marquis murmured.

"I suppose you thought your own friends would not mix with the locals," Elmina said, "and I expect you were right. But you cannot expect those who are left out not to feel envy, hatred and malice."

The Marquis sighed.

"Well, I suppose that is something we shall have to put right in the future. But I do promise you that apart from my Steeple-Chases, I had no idea I was expected to entertain people who were not my personal friends."

"Neighbours long to be neighbourly, and of course to see the glories of Falcon, and tell you how much they admire you!"

"I can hardly believe that!"

"But of course they do! They think you are over-whelming, arrogant, condescending but at the same time magnificent and of course a very exciting person to talk about."

"I asked you to tell me the truth, and I must believe that you have done so," the Marquis said somewhat ruefully. "But what we are much more concerned with, Elmina, are your feelings towards me."

She did not answer immediately and he went on.

"I realise now that I have been very remiss in not seeing more of you before we were married, but it never struck me for one moment, and I am being honest, that you were not delighted at the thought of being my wife. After all, you did say you would like to marry me."

"Yes, I said that," Elmina admitted, "and it was true, but I was really thinking of you as the owner of Falcon—and of course your wonderful horses!"

"You mean you wanted my title?"

"No, of course not!" she exclaimed. "I have ad-mired you for years when I saw you out hunting, and I always watched you secretly, riding in your Steeple-Chases. I knew then that no man in the world could ride as well as you!"

Her voice changed as she went on.

"But having heard so much about the . . . beautiful Ladies with whom you . . . spent your time, I realised I had . . . no chance at all of . . . competing with . . . them."

The Marquis looked at her sharply, as if he sus-

114

pected she was not telling him the truth, but he did not interrupt and Elmina continued.

"I therefore could only hope...while your offer to Papa to marry me...was made in such an...abrupt manner...that in time...I could...interest you as a person...and you might find me a...pleasant companion...and someone with whom to share your...interests."

She spoke hesitatingly, as if she were choosing her words with care, and the Marquis, listening intently, felt that in what she was saying there was a great deal left unsaid.

"What other interests?"

There was a little pause before Elmina replied:

"Do you really want to know...or are you just being...polite in asking me these questions?"

"I really want to know," the Marquis said finally. "I think, Elmina, it is essential that we be completely and absolutely honest with each other."

"I...I will try," she said simply. "Perhaps you will understand when I tell you that I have always been a...terrible disappointment since the moment I was...born."

"Why?"

"Because Papa so desperately wanted to have a son, and Mama was convinced before I actually arrived in the world that I...was a boy."

The way she spoke and the expression in her eyes told the Marquis how much she had suffered later in knowing of her parents' disappointment.

"It was not until I was nearly fourteen that Desmond arrived unexpectedly," she went on. "For some years previously Papa had been treating me as if I were a boy, and I was aware every minute of every day I was with him how much he resented the fact that I was only a girl!"

She gave a little sigh before she continued.

"It was then I began to realise that as I would never be as beautiful as Mirabel or Deirdre, the best thing I could do would be to try to be as intelligent as a man."

Again the Marquis looked at her as if he could hardly believe she was telling the truth.

Then he asked:

"And how did you set about that?"

"I think it was soon after I had first seen you riding in a Steeple-Chase, which of course you won, and I watched you every time you came out hunting."

"How old were you then?"

"Twelve or thirteen, and I was also beginning to hear about your love-affairs."

The Marquis's lips tightened, but he did not say anything and Elmina continued as if she were looking back into the past.

"I realised that my Governess, who was a very sweet woman but rather stupid, could not teach me any more than she had already. So I went to see the Vicar, who sometimes makes a little extra money by coaching young men before they go up to a University."

The Marquis was becoming more and more incredulous.

"Of course I could not pay him without Papa or

Mama finding out what I was doing," Elmina said, "and I was quite sure they would not approve, so I persuaded him to let me sit quietly in a corner of his Study when he was instructing his pupils, and he corrected my homework as he corrected theirs. He often said that if it were a competition, I would be the winner!"

Her voice softened and there was a sparkle in her green eyes as she said in a different tone of voice:

"I loved learning Greek and Latin, and as the Vicar was a Classical Scholar himself he always took the pupils who wanted to specialise in Classical subjects."

"And your father and mother had no idea this was going on?" the Marquis asked.

"I had to let my Governess into the secret, and because she was fond of me and agreed there was little more she could teach me, she let Papa and Mama think I was having lessons with her when actually I was at the Vicarage."

"This is the most extraordinary thing I have ever heard!" the Marquis exclaimed.

"It was wonderful for me, except when Papa eventually sent my Governess away and it became difficult for me to go to the Vicarage regularly. But the Vicar said he was absolutely certain that if I could have gone to Oxford or Cambridge I could easily take a Degree!"

"You said I was somehow concerned in this," the Marquis observed.

"You were concerned," Elmina explained, "because seeing you and admiring you, I thought perhaps one day I would find a man who was . . . like you and who would want to . . . marry me."

She gave him a shy little smile as she added:

"I never dreamt for one moment that I would...marry you...of course I did not! I was quite certain, as everybody else around here was, that you would choose a wife, when you wanted one, from the young ladies whom you met in London."

She said no more but waited for his comments.

"And then you learnt Karate," the Marquis remarked. "But the really important question is, what are you going to do about me?"

"I have thought about that, and that is what I wanted to tell you."

"Now I have no option but to listen to you."

He smiled as he spoke and as Elmina smiled back at him she said:

"I can only say once again that I am...sorry!"

"There is no need to apologise, but I do want to hear your suggestions for the future."

Elmina put her head a little to one side as she asked:

"What do you most enjoy doing in your life? What gives you the greatest pleasure?"

The Marquis thought an appropriate reply to the question could be, 'Making love,' but he felt in the circumstances it would be somewhat embarrassing.

Therefore, thinking quickly, he replied:

"It is difficult to answer, but perhaps winning a race in a close finish."

"Exactly!" Elmina cried. "In other words—you have had to strive and use your intelligence as well as your expertise."

She did not wait for him to answer but went on.

"It is the same with hunting. I know that to every

sportsman it is not catching and killing the fox which counts. The real enjoyment is having a good run— in fact the excitement of the chase!"

"Are you somehow applying these two exercises to us?" the Marquis asked.

"Yes, of course I am," Elmina replied. "I think, because you are you, it would be very unsatisfactory for you to have a wife whom you have not wooed and pursued with considerable effort, even with anxiety, in case she said 'No' instead of 'Yes.'"

The Marquis was silent after she had finished speaking. Then unexpectedly he laughed.

"Did you really think all this out for yourself?"

"I have given it a great deal of thought," Elmina replied, "and as you so often look bored and what Mirabel calls 'supercilious,' I am quite certain it is because everything in your life has come to you too easily. In fact what Chang says the Chinese call: *'The peach falling into open hand!'*"

"I realise exactly what you are saying to me," the Marquis remarked.

He knew as he spoke it was extremely perceptive of any woman, especially anybody as young as Elmina, to realise that often women melted into his arms before he had even held them out to them, and that the invitation he saw in every beautiful woman's eyes made even the most ardent love-affair seem somewhat unadventurous.

But it was astounding that Elmina could have thought all this out for herself.

Because he felt he must question her further he asked:

"Are you really saying to me that I have to chase you as if you were a fox, or win a race in which you are the prize, before you will consent to be my wife in anything but name?"

"You are making it sound rather different from the way I thought of it," Elmina answered. "What I was really thinking was that if we became friends—perhaps 'companions' is the better word—and you could get to know me, perhaps you would begin to like me as a person, and..."

She paused and there was a faint flush on her cheeks as if she were afraid to go any further.

"I would eventually fall in love with you," the Marquis finished. "Is that what you are really thinking, Elmina?"

She nodded, then clasped her hands together tightly and said:

"Please...I do not want to be difficult...and I am very, very sorry that instinctively I...protected myself against you...but I do want more from you than you are...offering me at the...moment."

She thought the Marquis did not understand and went on.

"You will think it very...ignorant of me...but I am not at all...sure what 'making love' between a man and a woman really...means. I think Mama and my sisters thought I was...too young to talk about it...then as we were married in such a... hurry...there was no time."

What she said to the Marquis was really incredible.

While he never expected that any pure young girl would have any experience of love-making, he had never dreamt that anyone he married would be completely ignorant.

"I am sure whatever happens could be...very wonderful," Elmina went on in a low voice. "At the same time I know from what I have read that it is something that should mean a very great deal to the bride and to the bridegroom. That is why I asked myself how, when you had seen me only a very few times, I could now mean anything...special to you."

The Marquis did not know what to say and she added:

"And yet...perhaps when you grow to know me...and if you were not too disappointed in my appearance...I could mean something...just a little different from all the other beautiful Ladies to whom you have...made love...but who have been unable to...hold you...and you have left them."

The Marquis drew in his breath.

He felt as if he were advancing deeper and deeper into a maze out of which he could not for the moment see his way clearly.

"I do understand what you are saying to me, Elmina," he said after a long pause, "and strangely enough, now I think about it, I see it is a sensible way for us both to approach our marriage."

"You understand...you really understand?" Elmina cried.

"I think I do," the Marquis answered, "and therefore all I can say is that we will give it a try."

Now Elmina's eyes were dazzling.

"Thank you, thank you. I was so afraid you would not understand...and I promise you I will try very hard to be ... exactly the wife you want ... and not disappoint you."

"I do not think you will do that," the Marquis said. "Now, if I agree to give your suggestion a try, will you promise me something else?"

"What is that?"

"That you will be completely frank and truthful about everything that concerns us both, and when you think I have won the race you will tell me so."

Elmina smiled.

"I think you will know that for yourself, and thank you very much for being so kind."

The Marquis rose to his feet.

"I am now going to bed, Elmina, to think over what we have said to each other. I want you to go to sleep so that you will not be tired tomorrow morning when we go riding."

"I shall not be tired, and I am looking forward to it very much."

As she looked up at him, her pale hair shining silver in the candlelight and her eyes seeming to glitter, the Marquis wondered if he should kiss her, then decided it was against the rules.

Instead he picked up her hand and just touched it with his lips.

"Good night, Elmina," he said, "and I look forward to racing you tomorrow in more ways than one!"

Elmina gave a little laugh.

"I shall do my very best to beat you."

The Marquis too was laughing as he left the room.

*   *   *

The next morning Elmina came downstairs when the hands of the grandfather clock in the hall showed it was slightly past seven-thirty.

She had thought she would be first, but the Marquis was already taking his tall hat from one of the footmen and she thought he looked particularly handsome wearing his white riding-breeches and shining boots.

She had been most particular in her choice of riding-habits for the trousseau.

Her mother was not in the least interested in these, so she had been able to choose three.

This seemed rather extravagant, but she knew that to herself they were far more important than gowns.

The one she was wearing this morning was a summer habit of dark blue silk material which was a perfect frame for her hair and white skin.

She had several lace-trimmed petticoats beneath the very full skirt and the closely-fitting jacket accentuated her figure and her very small waist.

Her blouse had a small bow at the neck which was of a paler blue than the habit itself.

The same colour was echoed in the gauze that surrounded her high-crowned hat and hung down her back.

She was however for the moment quite unconcerned with her appearance, thinking only of the Marquis and the horses that were waiting for them outside the front door.

A stable-boy was holding her horse while Hogson was in charge of Samson, the Marquis's stallion, and both grinned at her when she appeared.

"Good-morning, Hogson. Good-morning, Jim!" she said in a friendly way.

"Marnin' M'Lady!" Jim answered. "Skylark's real frisky this marnin'. 'E ain't bin exercised since the day afore yesterday, 'cause we ain't 'ad a minute to spare."

"I am glad about that!"

Elmina realised as she spoke that the Marquis coming down the steps behind her had heard the conversation and he said sharply:

"If Skylark is too much for you, there are plenty of quieter horses in my stables."

He looked at Hogson somewhat accusingly as he spoke, but the Head Groom, who was well aware that Elmina could ride anything and control any horse however obstreperous, said:

"Her Ladyship'll hold 'im, M'Lord!"

"I hope you are right," the Marquis said in an ominous tone.

Afraid that he might insist on her having a quieter animal, Elmina, without waiting for him to assist her into the saddle as he expected to do, seemed almost to fly into it without any help.

There was therefore nothing the Marquis could do but mount his own horse and ride ahead.

Elmina followed him, aware that Jim was right and Skylark was in a very skittish mood.

He was in fact, as Hogson knew, a horse for whom she had a great affection, and whenever she went to the stables, Skylark was the first horse she visited.

He had been almost uncontrollable before she had

made a regular practice of talking to him. Then by helping Hogson saddle him she had made him much more amenable than they had ever expected in so short a time.

She knew the reason why Hogson had brought Skylark for her the first day of her marriage was that he knew the horse meant so much to her. But the Marquis was not to know that they had ever met before.

Skylark performed his usual tricks, bucking and shying at everything that moved.

At the same time, with his ears back, he was listening to Elmina talking to him and telling him it was important that he should behave himself.

As soon as the Marquis, riding ahead, was free of the oak trees in the Park, he moved northwards and Elmina knew he was heading for the gallop.

This was on a level piece of land below, which was the ground he always used as a Steeple-Chase and from where she and Chang had watched the riders.

The sun was shining, the hay had already been cut, and the gallop was in perfect order for what she knew was to be a race between her and her husband.

He pulled in his horse to let her catch up with him, and she was aware that the reason for his going ahead had been to show the way across the Park.

Now he said:

"This is my gallop, Elmina. I think we should take some of the freshness out of Skylark."

"Of course!"

She dug her heel in lightly as she spoke and Skylark was off.

He leapt forward and it took the Marquis several seconds to catch up with her.

Then they were galloping neck and neck at a speed that seemed to blow the breath from between their lips.

It was as if the two horses knew instinctively it was a competition that was important to their riders.

Skylark strained every nerve in his body to keep ahead of the Marquis's stallion, which was in perfect condition and not used to being outrun by any other horse.

It was, in fact, Samson on which Elmina had seen him win the Steeple-Chase the previous winter.

For the moment however she could think of nothing but keeping Skylark under control and feeling almost deafened by the sound of the horses' hoofs thundering over the dry ground.

They reached the end of the gallop in what Elmina was certain must be record time.

As they passed a white post, which she knew was not only considered the winning-post but also a warning that they must draw in their horses, she could have sworn that there was not an inch between the two animals.

She accordingly began to tighten her reins on Skylark and she knew the Marquis was doing the same thing to Samson.

Then, as the two horses came down to a trot and she could breathe, she turned a laughing face towards her husband.

"I would like to claim that I won," the Marquis

said, "but as you well know I cannot do that!"

"I think it was a dead heat."

There was a lilt of excitement in her voice that he did not miss.

"I expected, as your father's daughter, that you would ride well, but I do not know any woman, or any man for that matter, who could have controlled Skylark as you did."

Elmina bent forward and patted the horse's neck.

"He is an old friend," she said without thinking, "and we understand each other."

Then as she realised what she had said she looked at the Marquis apprehensively.

"So you have seen my horses before!" he exclaimed. "I thought it was strange that you should know the stable-boys by name."

"Guilty, My Lord!"

"When have you visited my stables, and by whose invitation?"

Elmina then told him the story of how her horse had cast a shoe, and she had asked Hogson if the Blacksmith was available.

"And what happened after that?"

Elmina and the Marquis were now going slowly back the way they had come along the gallop, and he knew from the way she did not look at him that she was embarrassed.

"I imagine you went round the house. I thought last night it was strange that you were able to find your way to your bedroom without anybody's assistance."

"You are more observant than I expected!"

"I am not sure whether that is a compliment or an insult, or perhaps both."

"I admit I have been to Falcon on many occasions, so now you can understand that if I wanted to marry you for your horses, I also fell in love with your Library."

The Marquis laughed and it was a genuine sound of amusement.

"If you give me any more surprises, I shall have a heart-attack," he said. "Quite frankly, Elmina, I am beginning to be afraid of you!"

"I do hope not!" she said impulsively, then realised he was teasing her.

"To any suspicious-minded person it would appear that you decided to marry me long before I was aware you even existed."

"You can hardly think that, considering your letter came like a bolt out of the blue. When Papa read it he could not believe it was not a joke."

"Why should your father have been surprised? I had already discussed the matter with him at White's."

Elmina laughed.

"Papa had no idea what you said to him at the time. He told us there was a lot of noise coming from some of the younger members, and what was more, you were talking into his deaf ear!"

The Marquis laughed until the sound seemed to echo round them.

"Everything about you is unusual, Elmina," he remarked, "and it never entered my head that your father had not heard what I said."

"He knew what it was all about only when you put it in your letter."

"Then what happened?" the Marquis asked.

"When he read it aloud to us at breakfast, Mirabel said she loved Robert and intended to marry him, and Deirdre revealed for the first time that she was secretly engaged to Christopher Bardsley."

"So that left you."

"That left me," Elmina repeated, "and when I said that I would be willing to marry you, both Papa and Mama said I was too young. I think, although they did not say so, that they were thinking of your reputation."

She smiled at him provocatively, but before he could answer she rode ahead out of the gallop towards the Steeple-Chase course below them.

Because it was impossible for two people to ride side-by-side on the narrow pathway, the Marquis caught up with her only when she had reached the start of it.

"You are not to attempt to jump these fences," he said firmly. "They are too much for a woman."

Elmina did not answer. She only brought her whip lightly down on Skylark's flank and he moved off with the speed of a cannon-ball.

He had taken three of the fences before the Marquis was within speaking distance.

Then as Elmina expected him to order her to stop, he merely shouted as he galloped beside her:

"If I do not beat you this time, I will give up riding!"

It was a challenge she could not resist, and she

urged Skylark on, at the same time being careful at every fence, as she had no wish to fall, which would give the Marquis an undisputable victory.

But try as she could, and Skylark certainly did his best, he was just ahead of her at the last fence and Samson passed the winning-post at least half a length ahead.

She knew as they drew their horses to a standstill that the Marquis was delighted to have proved himself the victor, but he said to tease her:

"Not at all bad for a woman! But you must try to do better another time!"

"That is extremely ungenerous of you!" she retorted. "Skylark jumped just as well as Samson even though his legs are a little shorter!"

The Marquis's eyes twinkled as he said:

"You were both magnificent, as you know full well! Let us go home. I feel I have earned my breakfast the hard way!"

As they rode back Elmina thought she had never in her life enjoyed herself so much.

She had the feeling that, unless she was very much mistaken, the Marquis was already beginning to think about her in a very different way.

But she could not be sure of anything except that, thanks entirely to Chang, she had started off her marriage as she wanted to do.

Now she could only pray that by relying on her instinct and 'looking inwards' she could make it what she hoped. But she was half-afraid she was asking too much.

chapter six

ELMINA awoke with a feeling of happiness.

For a moment she thought it was time to get up, then realised it was still dark and there was no light coming from between the curtains.

She therefore lay thinking of how much she had enjoyed the first week of her marriage and how wonderful it had been.

She had had no idea it could be so entrancing to be alone with a man as clever and intelligent as the Marquis. Moreover, so many interesting things had happened that she hardly had time to think during the day.

When she went to bed at night she fell asleep almost as soon as her head touched the pillow.

The second day of their marriage, as if the Marquis had been thinking it over, he said:

"I am not only intrigued by the fact that you have learnt Karate, but also feel that it is extremely *infra dig* for me to be beaten physically by my wife in a combat of which I know absolutely nothing."

Elmina looked at him enquiringly as he went on.

"I therefore suggest that either you teach me this science at which you are so proficient, or we ask your instructor to do so."

"Do you mean that?" Elmina cried excitedly. "But of course Chang will teach you! I am only his pupil, and I have never yet beaten him in even the most elementary throws."

When the Marquis agreed, she thought it was the most thrilling thing that could happen, and she wrote a note to her father asking if she could borrow Chang for a few days.

She then wrote another note to Chang, telling him to bring his special clothes with him.

The Earl was rather puzzled by her request but felt it was something he could not refuse, and a few hours later Chang arrived.

The Marquis had instructed the Groom who took the note to lead a horse for Chang by which he could return.

In the meantime Elmina had arranged a room on the same floor as their bedrooms, which she learnt was not often used.

When she told the Housekeeper she wanted all the furniture removed and a number of mattresses put down on the floor, Mrs. Leonard was astounded.

"What can you want something like that for, M'Lady?" she enquired.

"His Lordship is thinking of building a Gymnasium," Elmina replied, having thought this out before. "In the meantime this will have to do for my special exercises, and I have no wish to slip on the polished floor."

"No, indeed not, M'Lady! I quite understand!" Mrs. Leonard said although Elmina was sure she was finding it very perplexing.

The Marquis said the first thing he wanted was to see his wife in combat with Chang.

She was so thrilled that he was interested that, when she put on the black pantaloons and the tunic she had made herself, she did not notice that the Marquis's eyes were twinkling when he looked at her and she therefore was not embarrassed.

Because she was completely unselfconscious, she had no idea that the Marquis had been amazed when he realised that once she was dressed in the morning she seldom, like other women, looked in a mirror, and never appeared to expect him to comment on her gowns.

Now that she was dressed to all intents and purposes as a boy, he saw how slim she was, and also admired the athletic suppleness of her body.

He sat in a chair at the side of the room and listened with close interest while Chang explained what was happening.

He learnt that first very great care must be taken to ensure that the hand in the shape of the fist was correctly formed.

"A loose fist, M'Lord, would suffer damage if the blow struck against an attacker!" Chang said.

He then showed the Marquis the *Seiken-Tsuki*, a blow to the solar plexus which Elmina parried cleverly and struck back at him.

What interested the Marquis particularly was the *Mae-Geri*, a blow with the ball of the foot. It was this blow which Elmina had used to knock him down on their wedding-night.

When Chang and Elmina demonstrated the *Mawashi-Geri*, a blow with the foot to an opponent's head, he knew it was something he had to learn.

Elmina was amused to notice that, while Chang had been almost subserviently respectful to the Marquis on first arrival, as soon as he began to teach, the way he spoke was firm and authoritative.

She knew that the spiritual side of Karate was to him of far greater importance than the physical exercise.

Rather to her surprise, the Marquis quickly understood and accepted this, and when he had been shown by Chang the special breathing techniques, he at once grasped the spiritual aspect of mental concentration.

'He is very, very clever,' she told herself as she saw him comprehending even more quickly than she had the inner meaning that was essentially the foundation of Karate.

This of course was derived from Bodhidharma, the monk who had originally taught it at the Shaolin Temple.

They worked hard for nearly two hours with Chang, then, leaving him with Hogson to show him the horses, the Marquis and Elmina again went riding.

Feeling they had exerted themselves enough for

one day, he took her quietly through the woods and she found herself entranced by the beauty of the trees and the quiet pools where the wild deer sprang away at their appearance.

Rare birds Elmina had never seen before fluttered to the tops of the trees before she really had time to observe them properly.

"My father was very interested in birds," the Marquis explained, "and at one time had a large aviary. Some of them escaped and have bred in the woods without apparently much difficulty."

"I think that is very exciting!" Elmina said. "But I should be afraid when your friends are shooting pheasants or partridges that they might kill some of these by mistake."

"Not if they wish to be invited another time!" the Marquis said sharply.

Elmina realised that no penalty could prove more effective.

At dinner they seemed to have so much to talk about that she was quite surprised to find the evening had passed and it was time for bed.

When they retired and the Marquis left her, as was now his custom, at the door of her bedroom, he said:

"The usual time, if you wish to come riding in the morning! Good-night, Elmina. I know you will sleep well."

"I hope you will also," she replied.

"I will doubtless dream that you are defeating me either on the jumps," he smiled, "or else with some new hold Chang has neglected to show me!"

She had laughed, but when she was in her bedroom

she felt suddenly very alone and wished she could go on talking to him.

"He is so intelligent," she told herself.

She said a little prayer of thankfulness that she found she could talk to him almost on equal terms.

She felt sometimes as if he deliberately introduced subjects that were beyond the comprehension of the average woman, almost as if he were trying to catch her out and prove her ignorant.

Very occasionally she had to admit that she did not understand what he was saying, but usually they had a spirited argument, perhaps about some obscure religion about which she knew as much as he did or over some point of Classical History.

Whatever it was, Elmina was aware that neither Mirabel nor Deirdre would have known anything about the subject, and she suspected that most of the Marquis's lady-friends would be no less ignorant.

She could not help wondering whether he missed Lady Carstairs.

Sometimes not when she was riding with him, but when they were sitting in the Salon after dinner, she longed to ask him if he preferred looking into the inviting blue eyes of the woman he loved rather than hers.

However honest they had promised to be with each other, she felt sure that his love-affairs were 'taboo' and he would consider it 'bad taste' on her part to mention them.

Now, lying in the dark, Elmina wondered, as she had wondered almost every night, what the Marquis felt about her, and if his feelings had changed in any way from the first night when he had come to her bedroom.

He had expected then to make love to her, although it could not have been, even for him, love as he had known it, and quite certainly not the very special spiritual experience she wanted it to be for herself.

Yet he must have felt some urge to touch her and kiss her, otherwise he would not have come.

Now, after a whole week together, he had shown no sign whatever of thinking of her as an attractive woman or in any way desirable.

'Perhaps I have lost him by being too clever,' Elmina thought.

Then to her surprise she found herself questioning whether she had been right in insisting on their marriage being so very different from what the Marquis had taken for granted.

Supposing she had let him make love to her, whatever that entailed, as he had expected to do?

Perhaps then he would have fallen in love with her instead of, as she now realised, treating her on her own insistence, as a companion, and a male one at that!

"Have I been stupid? Have I thrown away the substance for the shadow?" she asked herself.

She felt lost, alone, very young and hopelessly ignorant.

What did she know of men, especially one like the Marquis?

How could she have compelled him to change his mind and to make it on her own terms impossible for him now to approach her?

"I have been a fool!" she told herself, and wanted to cry.

She had an irresistible impulse to go into his bedroom, wake him up and ask him to be frank with her.

Suppose she did that and said to him:

"I have made a mistake! Please want me as you did on the night we were married! Let us start from there, rather than worry as to whether it is the ideal love or something very different."

Then she told herself that everything in which she believed and everything that Chang had taught her made her sure that the love that was worth having was something one must strive for.

It came not only from the heart and the body, but also from the soul.

"But why should the Marquis believe that?"

The question seemed to dance in front of her eyes.

Then, because she was so agitated by the ideas that seemed to come flooding into her mind, frightening her with their intensity, she got out of bed and walked to the window.

She slipped behind the curtains as she had done the first night of her marriage and stood looking out over the garden and the lake beyond.

Now the moon was on the wane, but there was still enough light from what was left of it and from the stars to see the beauty of everything below her.

But instead of its loveliness lifting her up into the sky as it usually did, she felt a dull ache of fear that she would never find what she sought, and to the Marquis she would never be anything very special.

138

'I love him!' she thought, and was astonished to find herself realising it. 'I want him to love me as a man loves a woman who to him is different from all other women!'

She told herself despairingly that would never happen and was startled by the pain that seemed to seep through her whole body at the thought.

Suddenly she felt she could not bear the loneliness of the great room with its golden cupids symbolic of the love which was eluding her.

In the same way as when she had been at home, she felt her only comfort could be found with the horses.

As she thought of it she knew it would be exciting to look again at the horse which had arrived only yesterday and which the Marquis intended to ride to-morrow.

Two days ago he had given an exclamation of excitement when a letter had arrived by post.

"What is it?" she asked.

"I have a surprise for you," he answered, "and one which I feel will give you as much pleasure as it gives me."

"What is it?" Elmina asked again curiously.

"I have bought an Arab mare which is considered by the experts to be the most outstanding horse in the world!"

Elmina's eyes had lit up and the Marquis had gone on.

"She belongs to an Arab Chieftain to whom I did a good turn a long time ago. When I heard about the

139

mare, I wrote to him asking that, if ever he considered selling her, he would allow me the privilege of being her owner."

"And did he say 'yes'?"

"He replied with the flowery sentiments of the East that he would be honoured that Shalom, which is the name of the mare, should grace my stables."

The Marquis paused to look down again at the letter. Then he said:

"I did not tell you about it, because the Arabs are invariably unpredictable, and I thought that while he agreed to my suggestion, he might easily find innumerable excuses for not sending the mare away from his own country."

The Marquis held out the letter to her.

"I was wrong. As you see, this is to inform me that Shalom has actually arrived at Dover, and Allah willing, will be here in two days' time."

Elmina had been almost as excited as the Marquis and when the mare had arrived yesterday evening as dusk was falling they had both gone to the stables to see her safely ensconced in the stall which had been prepared for her.

She was a beautiful animal with an arched neck and all the characteristics of a pure-bred Arab mare.

She was so faultless that Elmina could understand her being spoken of as 'the most perfect horse in the world.'

It had been impossible, to the Marquis's great annoyance, to keep such a purchase secret from the newspapers.

They not only reported the mare's arrival, but also

had described his house and his stables and had made some very complimentary comments about the other horses he possessed.

Elmina had read the articles in both *The Times* and the *Morning Post* and had remarked:

"I am sure this will mean we shall have sightseers knocking on the gates and asking to see Shalom."

"I am extremely annoyed that I should be written about in such a way!" the Marquis replied. "I dislike publicity of any sort, for it invariably ends in trouble."

Remembering how the local people had talked about him and Lady Carstairs, Elmina quickly changed the subject.

She was certain she was right, and whether they were on their honeymoon or not, people would certainly call and ask if they could see Shalom.

Now, knowing she would find it impossible to sleep, she thought she would pay a quick visit to the stables, which was something she had often done at home whatever the time of night.

She lit a candle and opened her wardrobe to find something to wear. The first thing she saw lying on the floor of the cupboard was the black suit she wore for Karate.

It was easier to slip into this than into anything else, and as she was certain there would be nobody to notice her, she took off her nightgown and put on the two garments.

Tying back her long hair with a ribbon, she opened the door of her bedroom very quietly and walked down the passage.

As usual at night, the majority of the candles in

their silver sconces had been extinguished, but there were a few alight so that it was easy for her to find her way.

Elmina however did not go down the main staircase, knowing the night-footman would be on duty in the hall.

Instead she took a secondary staircase which led her to a garden-door from which she had only to walk a short distance through a number of rhododendron bushes to reach the entrance to the stables.

There was enough light in the sky to see her way, and yet in the shadows she was quite certain if there was anybody looking out, they would not notice her.

She had no wish to explain why she was so restless in the middle of the night.

There was a large archway leading into the cobbled yard of the stables through which she passed and, as she expected, everything was quiet.

Although she knew there were always one or two of the stable-lads on duty at night in case any of the horses was ill or frightened, she expected they would be asleep and would not hear her.

The outside door of the stable was open, which rather surprised her.

Then as she went inside she was just about to go first into the stall occupied by Skylark when she realised there was a light in the next one in which Shalom had been housed.

She went quickly to it, found the door open, and walked in to see with astonishment there were two men whom she did not recognise with the Arab mare.

142

They turned round as she appeared and one of them in a rough voice exclaimed:

"Who are yer an' wot d'yer want?"

"It's a woman!" the other one said.

"What are you doing here...?" Elmina began to ask.

Then as she spoke something heavy was thrown over her head from behind her, and even as she began to struggle she realised she was helpless.

She wanted to scream, but her voice was lost against the thickness of the horse-blanket and her arms beneath it were roped down to her sides.

A rope was put around her ankles, tying them together, and then as she screamed in fear she was toppled over and laid down on the floor.

It had all happened so quickly, and she was trussed up like a chicken almost before she had time to think.

"Ye said as 'ow ye'd knocked 'em all out, Bert," one man said.

"I 'as! This woman weren't 'ere then!"

"Tiens! Wot we do wiv her?" another voice asked.

Elmina had the idea it was the man who had come up behind her and thrown the horse-blanket over her.

She thought he spoke with a strange accent which was unlike that of the other two men.

"Better take 'er wiv us," the first one who had spoken said. "She's seen our faces so it wouldn't be safe to leave 'er 'ere."

"Easier kill 'er!"

The way the other man spoke made Elmina draw in her breath with fear.

"Us'll go into that later. Come on! Abe said get a move on!"

"If we've gotta take 'er, we'll need another 'orse."

"Orl right, Bert, but take a quiet 'un and ye can have 'er in front of ye. 'T'll be easier that way, an' I'll ride th' Arab."

Elmina listened with horror.

She realised the men were thieves who had come to steal the Arab mare because she had been described in the newspapers as being the most perfect horse in the world.

She was also the most expensive, which meant that somebody had employed these men to steal Shalom from the Marquis.

She heard footsteps as one of the men went to the next stall and she knew he was inspecting Skylark.

Then as the horse, who always resented strangers in his stall, lashed out at him, Bert came back quickly saying:

"I ain't takin' that animal!"

"Then find 'nother, ye fool!" the man who was obviously in charge replied. "There's enough of 'em to choose from!"

Bert walked in the opposite direction and a minute later said:

"There's one that seems quiet enough down 'ere, but oi wants some 'elp in saddling 'im."

"Bring that one then," Abe said. "Jacques can help ye!"

It was he who had first spoken to Elmina, and she thought now he had seemed almost middle-aged, but she was sure he was experienced with horses.

There was something that was, she knew, very noticeable in men who were Grooms and Jockeys and had always spent their lives with horse-flesh.

He was obviously having no trouble in putting a saddle on Shalom. The mare was standing still while he did so, and Elmina thought that was not only because the animal was tired after her long journey.

She herself was more frightened than she had ever been before in her life.

She was quite certain that these men would not hesitate to kill her if it suited them, and she had no chance of defending herself when she could not move either her hands or her feet.

She heard the two men who were farther down the stable coming back, bringing a horse with them.

She fancied, although she could not be sure, that it was one of the horses the Marquis had had for some years and which he rode out hunting.

"Ye ready, Abe?" the man called Bert asked.

Abe, who had now saddled Shalom replied:

"Oi be ready! Jacques can ride one of 'em us came on!"

"They bain't as good as these!"

"Take th' lot o' 'em then. Ye only needs four legs ter carry us ter th' coast!"

As he spoke Elmina understood.

They were taking Shalom abroad, and she guessed the instructions to steal her had come from one of the French owners. Now she recognised the accent of the third man: he was French!

The Marquis had told her during their various discussions how his greatest rivals on the race-course were the French.

"They send their best horses over here to try to beat me," he said, "but so far they have always failed!"

"Have you ever raced in France?" Elmina had enquired.

"Once or twice," he replied, "and I intend to try again next season. But I want to be quite certain before I do so that any horse I put into one of their races will win!"

Elmina had laughed.

"I think it is unsporting to bet on a certainty!"

"I feel I am racing not only on my own behalf but for the glory of England," he answered.

He spoke with the sarcastic note in his voice which he used so frequently.

Elmina had realised however that while he was mocking at his own patriotism he was actually very sincere.

Other apparently incidental remarks he had made at various times had made her suspect intuitively that he had built up a defensive attitude towards the world, as if he were afraid it might hurt him.

Perhaps, she told herself later that evening when she was alone, that was why he had avoided or deliberately had not sought the real love that meant so much to her.

It seemed hard to believe, but it might have been because he was afraid that having found it, he would be disappointed, and it was a risk he was not prepared to take.

It did not seem quite in keeping with what she had learnt of the rest of his character, and yet she asked herself humbly what did she really know about him?

For that matter, what did she know about men in general? He might be far more subtle and sensitive than she had suspected.

So Shalom was being stolen away to France, and the Marquis in consequence would lose not only his money but, what was important, a horse that was to have been the most shining jewel in his stable.

"How can I . . . stop it? How can I . . . help him?" Elmina tried to ask.

Because there was nothing else she could do, she simply prayed fervently for help.

As she did so she felt one of the men pull on the rope where it bound her ankles. She was sure it was Jacques who had put it on in the first place.

It was a relief to be free, to that extent, and she wondered if she should kick out at him, but knew that not being able to see, she would miss, and would only be tied up again.

It was then that a man—it was Abe—picked her up in his arms and carried her out of Shalom's stall and into the yard.

The horse which belonged to the Marquis was obviously standing there, and she felt herself lifted astride the saddle.

"Ye get oop behind her, Bert," Abe said, "an' if ye're not comf'table ye can sling 'er into the bushes after we've got well away from this place."

"'Er might still tell on we, if oi does that," Bert replied.

There was a short pause before Abe said:

"Ye're right! We'd best take 'er wi' us an' drop 'er in the sea. Then 'er can talk to th' fishes!"

He gave a chuckle at his own joke but was obviously afraid to laugh out loud in case he might be overheard.

He walked away, back into the stables.

Then there was the sound of hoofs and Shalom came into the yard and Elmina heard Abe say in a whisper:

"'Urry up! An' get going!"

Elmina felt Bert climbing into the saddle behind her, then picking up the reins he pulled her roughly back against him.

She was balanced somewhat precariously on the front of the saddle and knew it would be easy to fall off and hurt herself.

She therefore held fast onto the horse's sides with her knees, thankful she was wearing pantaloons instead of a skirt, which would have obliged her to ride side-saddle.

Moving slowly with, she was sure, Abe leading the way on Shalom, they started to leave the stable-yard while the Frenchman came behind.

* * *

The Marquis was also awake, having been unable to sleep because he had been thinking of the Arab mare's arrival and the things he and Elmina had been doing together all day.

He had found himself every night after going to

bed thinking over the conversations they had had and being more and more astounded by the quickness of her intellect.

He was continually surprised by the extent of knowledge their talks revealed in so young a woman.

He was in fact certain the Vicar had not been flattering Elmina when he told her that if she had been able to go to a University, she would have gained a good Degree.

The Marquis, unlike most of his contemporaries, had worked hard when he was at Oxford simply because he enjoyed learning and liked to both work and play.

He took part in the games, he was a member of the Bullingdon Club and he undoubtedly drank a great deal more than was good for him.

At the same time he took a great deal of exercise and also pleased his Tutors.

It was, in fact, at Oxford that he had first learnt to organise himself so that he did not waste time, which he considered rather precious, but filled every hour of the day to his own satisfaction.

He had however found in the Social World his knowledge was not put to any particular use, and if the conversation at Buckingham Palace was boring and banal, the same might be said of most of the dinner-parties that took place in the great houses of the aristocracy.

There were however exceptions, and he found himself in the first years after his accession to the title spending his time with older and more intelligent women simply because they interested him.

They in their turn had found him unusually intelligent and very different from the average man of his age.

Then of course he became captivated by the beauty of first one lovely lady then another.

Because they were all married, they were usually a few years older than he was, and although he learnt from them a lot about love, it was an emotion which came from their hearts and not from their minds or what Elmina would have described as their souls.

When he grew older the Marquis found it more interesting to entertain senior politicians, especially statesmen who had a knowledge of Foreign Affairs.

These naturally included Ambassadors representing their own countries in London and at least once a month he gave a dinner-party at Falcon House in Park Lane where there were no women guests present and the conversation was on a very high intellectual level.

He had felt during this first week of his marriage that although it seemed hardly credible, Elmina would not have been out of place at any of these special dinners.

In fact, he was quite certain that whatever the subject under discussion, she would be able to contribute to it.

He could never remember talking in the same way to any other woman, except those he had first known after he left Oxford.

He sometimes wondered when he and Elmina had sparred in words and he had to admit at the end of an argument that the honours were almost equal, whether he would ever find himself really at a loss and have to concede she was the winner.

He had not forgotten the lesson she had inflicted on him the first night of their marriage.

It gave him great satisfaction to realise that as far as Karate and Ju Jitsu were concerned, he was growing more proficient day by day, and that Chang, who was a very hard task-master, was undoubtedly delighted with his prowess.

"You have a natural aptitude, M'Lord," he had said today after their lesson, "and it is certainly a pleasure to find anybody as strong and healthy as Your Lordship!"

"Thank you," the Marquis replied.

He knew that he had pleased Chang in that he had not questioned the precepts which he had said were essential for understanding the science and the spirituality behind the exercises.

Nor had he doubted the importance of the special breathing technique, and, as Chang said firmly, Karate begins and ends with courtesy.

It had surprised Elmina that the Marquis had been so ready to bow to his opponent before they began to fight, and to also bow in gratitude when it was over.

Now, as the horse on which she was riding began to carry her farther and farther away from Falcon, she thought for the first time that perhaps she could reach the Marquis with thought.

It was thought, Chang had told them both, that was behind every blow they struck, every movement they made.

It was thought too which made them predict what

their opponent would do and was part of the religious significance for which Karate had been conceived in the first place.

Now, feeling desperately afraid and helpless, she prayed, trying to reach the Marquis to make him understand the danger she was in.

Then as she thought she might die and never see him again, she cried out to him despairingly and with an intensity that seemed to come from every nerve and from every part of her body.

"Help me! Save me!"

Even as she sent all her vibrations and her thoughts winging like arrows towards him, she also thought of Chang and prayed that he too would hear her.

* * *

The Marquis lit the candles beside his bed and told himself that if he could not sleep, he might as well read.

He had brought up from the Library, although he had not told Elmina so, a book on Buddhism, because the way she had spoken of it had told him it was closely linked with what she felt about Karate.

Because it was a long time since he had read anything so erudite, he was studying it very slowly, determined to understand every sentence, and trying too, although he would hardly admit it to himself, to find the inner meaning behind the words.

Then as he did so he found Elmina's face interfering with what his brain was trying so hard to assimilate.

Every day he had found himself wondering how she managed to look so different from any other woman. What was it, he asked, that made her hair, her eyes, the curves of her lips, seem not only so unusual but beautiful?

He could not help wondering whether she would seem sensational in London, or whether her beauty, which was very soft and not spectacular, would be lost there.

Then he knew it was not only her beauty which was haunting him but what lay behind it.

He had never known a woman both so intelligent and so full of personality, who because she was very young and completely unselfconscious was entirely unaware of it.

At first he had thought her modesty and what seemed to him a personal indifference must be a very clever act.

Then he knew it was not only utterly natural, but sprang from the fact that she had never been noticed because of her two beautiful elder sisters, and also, as she had explained, she had been unloved.

He found himself thinking of her all through the day in one way or another.

Only at night did he find it increasingly difficult not to go to her bedroom and, although he told himself it was just to talk to her, he knew he wanted very much more.

"Dammit! We cannot go on like this!" he said suddenly, shutting his book with a snap.

As he was wondering whether Elmina would be

shocked if he woke her up, there came a knock on his door.

At first he thought he must be mistaken, then the knock came again and he said:

"Come in!"

He could not imagine who could be disturbing him at this hour of the night.

The door opened and he saw it was Chang.

"What is it, Chang?" he asked. "Is something wrong with the horses?"

"Maybe, M'Lord, I not know. But I think, though I may be mistaken, for which I most humbly apologise, that Her Ladyship calls."

"Calls?" the Marquis asked sharply. "I did not hear her!"

Chang came a little farther into the room, one hand over the other, his arms pressed against his sides as he bowed very low.

"Master, forgive inopportuneness of this miserable servant, but I feel My Lady call, am afraid of danger."

As always when Chang was very moved, he became more Chinese in the way he expressed himself than English.

For a moment the Marquis hesitated.

He wondered if the servant was talking nonsense.

At the same time, there was something about Chang which told him, if nothing else, that he spoke with an unmistakable sincerity.

"We will soon see if you are right or wrong," he said.

He got out of bed as he spoke, and without putting

on his robe walked to the communicating door which led into Elmina's bedroom.

He opened it softly, hoping that if she was asleep he would not disturb her.

He had forgotten that if so, the room would be in darkness, and the moment he saw a lighted candle beside the bed he felt that something was indeed wrong.

Then he saw that the bed, which she had turned back, was empty, and as his eyes moved around the room he could see her nightgown lying in a heap by the wardrobe.

He knew then that Chang indeed was right.

As he turned back into his bedroom, Chang was already taking some clothes from the wardrobe with which he could dress himself.

As he did so, the Marquis found himself wondering frantically what could have happened.

At the same time, he knew that if, as Chang had said, although it seemed inconceivable, Elmina was in danger, then somehow he had to save her.

As he hurried into his clothes and quickly tied a silk handkerchief like a scarf around his neck, he knew that she was far more precious to him than he had yet admitted to himself.

In fact, he not only wanted her as a woman, but for what now seemed to him to be a long time, he also loved her.

chapter seven

As the Marquis and Chang reached the stables, Hogson came running towards them.

"M'Lord, I were just acomin' to find ye!" he shouted agitatedly. "Someone's stolen th' Arab mare, and two o' our other 'orses as well!"

He was so breathless that he was almost incoherent, and as the Marquis walked into the stables Hogson walked along behind him saying:

"They knocked out th' two lads who were on duty, M'Lord. It were me little son as sees 'em out th' window."

The Marquis had reached the empty stall where Shalom had been stabled as Hogson went on.

"''E were wakened by the noise they makes, an' 'e says when they rode off they had a young boy with 'em wrapped in a horse-cloth!"

The Marquis was suddenly still.

"A boy?" he queried.

"Me son say 'e had on long, tight trousers, M'Lord!"

The Marquis for a moment wondered helplessly what he could do.

Then Chang who had walked into the empty stall exclaimed:

"It's Frenchmen who are th' thieves, M'Lord!"

"How do you know that?" the Marquis asked sharply.

Chang held up the rope which had been tied around Elmina's ankles.

"In French stables they tie ropes in knots like this, M'Lord. This was not tied by Englishman!"

The Marquis turned to Hogson.

"How long ago did your son see the men leave?"

"Not long, M'Lord. Couldn't 'ave been much over ten minutes."

"Saddle Samson!"

The Marquis's order seemed to ring out in the stables.

As he spoke Chang ran to the next stall and started to saddle one of the other horses.

He was so quick that he was in the yard before Hogson had Samson ready for the Marquis, who swung himself into the saddle.

"Bring three of your men, Hogson," he ordered, "and follow me!"

Then he rode off.

He knew as Chang did that if the thieves were intending to get the mare over to France, they would make for the nearest point on the coast and ride directly south.

This meant they would pass through the Park over the gallop and down into the valley where the Marquis held his Steeple-Chases.

He reckoned that with the horses they had stolen, Samson would be able to overtake them. Moreover, the thieves were encumbered by Elmina, although he could not bear to think about that.

He supposed she must have disturbed them and rather than knock her out as they had the stable-boys they had taken her with them.

He did not underestimate the terror she must be suffering, nor the likelihood that the thieves would injure or even kill her.

It was then he knew that if he lost her, he would be losing something so precious, so unique and unusual that nothing could ever compensate him for such a loss.

"How can I have let this happen?" he asked.

He knew that following the publicity there had been in the newspapers, he had been very remiss in not foreseeing that the Arab mare might be stolen by one of his rivals on the race-course.

It seemed incredible, but he knew now when he thought about it that it was something which had happened before, although not to anybody as important as himself.

Gypsies stole horses and altered their appearance in order to cheat purchasers and the general public.

Horses had been disguised so as to run as novices

at a high price in the betting in races they had won before.

But he could not remember when last an owner as important as himself had lost a horse as fine or as valuable as Shalom.

He was furious at the thought that the story would make the headlines in the newpapers that were read by everybody who was interested in racing.

At the same time that did not really matter.

Nothing mattered except that he must find Elmina and save her from the men who had carried her away.

They reached the end of the Park and as they rode onto the gallop the Marquis spurred Samson forward, although the great stallion needed no encouraging.

He knew he was racing against time and he wondered if Chang riding beside him felt the same.

He was sure that Elmina was calling him by the power of thought which she had been taught in her Karate lessons.

'Dammit!' the Marquis said to himself. 'I will kill these devils for doing this to her!'

*   *   *

Elmina had a very uncomfortable ride down the long incline from the gallop into the valley below.

As her arms were not free, she could only attempt to keep steady in the saddle by pressing her knees on the sides of the horse and could not help falling forward.

Only Ben's arm around her waist prevented her from banging her face on the horse's neck or slipping off altogether.

He kept loosening his grip, then dragging her roughly backwards, which was very painful.

Then as they reached the flat ground he said:

"Oi can't stand this any longer! If yer wants to take this woman with ye, 'ave her on yer 'orse!"

No one answered and he added:

"She's making the goin' slower an' that could be dangerous!"

"*C'est vrai!*" the Frenchman exclaimed. "We go slow, they catch us! Hurry, *mes amis! Vite! Vite!*"

"Oi ain't 'avin' 'er talkin' abaht us!" Abe said.

"No, 'cors not!" Bert agreed. "We'd best kill 'er. Ye've got yer pistol with ye!"

He made as if to pull in his horse and Abe said:

"Not 'ere, yer fool! There's a river we crossed to get 'ere. We can chuck 'er body in there and ten to onc they won't find 'er 'til we're at sea."

"Good idea!" Bert agreed.

He spurred his horse forward as he spoke, although they were already travelling at a fast pace, and Elmina thought her last hope had gone.

She had deliberately not tried to scream or struggle, because she knew that all her thoughts must concentrate on alerting the Marquis and Chang to the danger she was in.

Now she knew that if they did find her she would be dead.

She wondered if the Marquis would much mind or if he would go for consolation to Lady Carstairs and just forget her.

'Save me! Save me!' she cried silently, knowing that if she screamed her voice would be lost against the thick horse-cloth.

She remembered the stream on the flat land beyond where the Marquis held his Steeple-Chases.

Although the river in the winter was often swollen, at this time of the year there would not be enough water in it to cover her body, so it would be easy for anybody crossing the stream to see her floating there.

But by that time she would be dead, and to be found would be a poor consolation.

Once again she prayed desperately that the Marquis would come to her aid.

'I love you! I love you!' she cried in her heart. 'You will never know now of my love...or that I have thought and dreamt of you for...years!'

Then she told herself that even if he did know, it would mean nothing to him.

At the same time, she wished that instead of erecting a barrier between herself and her husband, she had at least let him kiss her once, which would be something to think of as she was dying.

She felt the horse beneath her being pulled in and she cried out again with every nerve in her body:

"Save me! Save me!"

It was as if she could see the Marquis's handsome face in the darkness in front of her eyes, and she felt too that Chang was with him and she could see him also.

Surely he had been right in saying that thought was more important than anything else and that properly directed there was nothing that thought could not do.

"Save me! Save me!" she cried again, and knew

as Bert pulled in the reins of his horse it was now too late.

He dismounted and dragged her from the saddle.

"'Ere's the river!" he said. "It don't look more than a trickle to me, so wot are ye goin' to do with 'er?"

"Shoot 'er," Abe said, "but not with that cloth over her 'ead. It's be too thick."

"Yer mean oi'm to take it orf?" Bert asked.

Abe did not deign to answer and Elmina thought he was loading his pistol.

Standing where Bert had put her when he had taken her from the saddle, she was aware he was tugging at the rope which bound her.

"'Ere, Jacques!" he called. "Oi can't undo this damn' rope. Ye tied it, ye untie it!"

"Oui, oui!" the Frenchman agreed. "I do!"

Elmina was aware that he was walking towards her.

He must have led his horse along with him, for she could hear it breathing.

She felt the rope that encased her being unwound, and either Jacques or Bert pulled off the heavy horse-cloth which covered her head.

For a moment it was a relief to breathe the air and feel it cool on her face.

She had forgotten it would be dark, but there was moonlight and the stars and she could see clearly.

It took her a few minutes to focus her eyes, then she realised she was standing by the edge of the stream and the three men were staring at her.

163

She recognised Abe from the quick glance she had had of him in the stall, and also Bert.

Jacques was exactly what she would have expected a Frenchman to be like, small and dark, and she was quite certain a Jockey by profession.

They were all roughly dressed, and they had unmistakably the look of men who spent their lives constantly with horses.

Abe was, as she had suspected, loading his pistol.

He had one arm through Shalom's rein, and the Arab mare seemed unperturbed by what was happening and was standing quietly.

Elmina recognised Bert's horse on which she had ridden as Wellington, one of the Marquis's favourite hunters.

As if he sensed something was amiss, he was restless, moving his feet first one way, then another, until Bert, holding his bridle, gave it a sharp tug that made him throw up his head.

Jacques's horse was on the other hand very obstreperous and it was all he could do to keep it under control. But Elmina only gave him a quick glance before her eyes went back to Abe and the pistol he held in his hand.

She was aware of how strange she must look in her black tunic, with her hair loosened by the horse-cloth, falling over her shoulders.

Then as she thought of appealing to the men, she realised they were criminal types to whom life meant very little. She knew it would only be a waste of time, and she would not lower herself.

She therefore held her head high.

Unexpectedly the Frenchman said:

"Quelle jolie femme! We take wiv us!"

From the way he spoke it was quite obvious what he was thinking and Abe said sharply:

"We ain't got time fer that sort o' thing! Ye can 'ave all the women in France with th' money ye'll get for this lot!"

As if the word 'money' were far more convincing than any other argument, the Frenchman shrugged his shoulders.

But the way he was looking at Elmina made her feel slightly sick.

Then Abe cocked the pistol and asked:

"Ye ready, Lady? It'll be quick an' sharp an' ye won't feel a thing. That's wot they tells I!"

He smiled as he raised the pistol, ready to bring it down and take aim.

As he did so, Elmina, almost as if Chang were beside her telling her what to do, took action.

She moved forward so swiftly and unexpectedly that Abe had no idea what was coming.

Her foot shot out like a bar of iron, striking him on exactly the right place on his body to knock him backwards.

He fell and as he did so he instinctively pulled the trigger.

The bullet went harmlessly up into the air, but the noise of the explosion terrified the animals.

All three wrenched themselves free and with a clatter of hoofs careered down the field.

Bert, who was nearest to Elmina, hit out at her, knocking her to the ground, but even as she fell she heard in the distance the sound of hoofs, which were not made by the three that had run away.

Then she knew that the Marquis had heard her prayers and was on his way to save her.

He came towards them like a whirlwind, just as Abe was pulling himself up from the ground and swearing with a foulness which polluted the air around them.

As he got to his feet, the pistol still in his hand, the Marquis literally threw himself from his horse.

He pulled Abe to the ground and a second later Chang had landed on Bert, knocking him unconscious with a sharp blow at the neck, which if Elmina had seen it she would have known was part of Kung Fu.

Lying on the ground, she had eyes only for the Marquis.

He knocked Abe unconscious and came towards her to lift her to her feet.

She did not see Chang go after the Frenchman and knock him out in the same way as he had Bert.

All she could see was the Marquis's eyes as he looked at her.

"Are you all right?"

As he spoke he lifted her to her feet, and suddenly in reaction at finding herself saved, she burst into tears.

She flung herself against him and hiding her face against his shoulder sobbed:

"They . . . were going to . . . kill me!"

The Marquis held her very tightly, gently smoothing her hair.

"It is all right," he said quietly. "It is all right."

"I . . . I thought I . . . should never . . . see you again!"

"I am here."

He put his fingers under her chin and turned her face up to his.

In the light of the moon her hair was silver and he could see the tears both in her eyes and running down her cheeks.

Her black tunic had been torn as she struggled in the stable to try to prevent herself from being tied up.

And yet as he looked down at her he thought she had never looked more lovely.

Then, as if he could not help himself, he pulled her closer still and his lips came down on hers.

For a moment Elmina thought it could not really be happening.

Then as she felt a shaft of lightning sweep through her body she was free and the Marquis said:

"Let us get out of this mess! I will take you home."

As he spoke he was aware that coming down the field were a number of horsemen led by Hogson.

He did not take his arms from around Elmina; he merely waited for Hogson to ride up beside him.

The Groom dismounted, looked at the three men unconscious on the ground at the Marquis's feet and said with a grin:

"Oi sees Your Lordship 'as coped very adequately with them thieves!"

"I will leave them for you to bring back, Hogson," the Marquis replied, "and we will take them before the Magistrates later in the day."

"If I have my way, they'll all be hanged, M'Lord!" Hogson said savagely.

The Marquis glanced down at the horse-cloth at his feet which had covered Elmina.

"Put that horse-cloth on the front of my saddle," he said.

"Very good, M'Lord."

Hogson picked up the horse-cloth, folded it and put it over the front of the saddle. The Marquis lifted Elmina onto it.

Now she was sitting sideways, but even so she felt slightly embarrassed at the way she must have looked.

The Marquis however mounted quickly and without saying any more started to ride back the way they had come.

With a deep sigh of relief, Elmina put her head against his shoulder and closed her eyes.

It was hard to believe that she was really safe and had avoided being killed only at the very last moment.

If the Marquis and Chang had not arrived when they had, Abe would certainly have shot her with a second bullet, not only because she was a dangerous encumbrance, but also because he was furious at her having knocked him down.

Her swiftness in applying her knowledge of Karate had saved her life for just long enough to allow the Marquis and Chang to arrive in the nick of time.

"I am . . . safe," she told herself beneath her breath.

As if he knew what she was thinking, the Marquis's arm tightened around her.

He did not speak and in a way she was glad.

After the agony through which she had passed, she felt almost too limp to move her lips.

All that mattered was that she was close to the

Marquis. She could feel his heart beating and knew that he was there.

He was taking his horse slowly back up the incline which led to the gallop. Then when they reached the top of it and he could see her clearly before they went under the trees in the Park, he said:

"You are sure you are all right? How could you have done anything so mad as to go to the stables alone at night?"

"How could I have known...how could I have...guessed those thieves were...trying to steal Shalom away?"

"It is something that will never happen again!"

His lips were very close to hers and she thought he might kiss her again. She longed for him to do so, beseeching him with her eyes.

"We will talk about it when we get home," he said.

They rode on, and now she was no longer limp but vitally aware of him. At the same time she could not help thinking that perhaps he had kissed her on the spur of the moment and would not do so again.

It took the Marquis only a few minutes to ride through the Park and up to the front door.

There were two stable-boys waiting for them and as they ran to Samson's head the Marquis said:

"Hogson may need your help. Both of you can join him and take with you a roll of rope. Do you understand?"

"Yes, M'Lord!" they both said eagerly.

The lilting note in their young voices made it obvious that they were longing to be where the action was taking place.

The night-footman held the door open, but otherwise the house was quiet, for the other servants had not been alerted.

The Marquis lifted Elmina down from his saddle, and without putting her down carried her in his arms up the steps.

He entered the hall and continued up the stairs still with her close against his heart.

She thought it was the most wonderful thing that had ever happened to her and put her head against his shoulder, thinking that whatever the future held for her she would have this to remember.

She was close to him, and for one magical, entrancing moment he had kissed her.

They reached her bedroom and the door was ajar, as she had left it.

He carried her inside and as he put her down gently he said:

"Get into bed."

Instinctively, because she did not wish him to leave her, Elmina put out her hands and he added:

"I will come back in a moment to talk to you."

She smiled at him in the candlelight and he shut the door into the passage, then went through the communicating door into his own bedroom.

Because he had said he would come back Elmina hurriedly pulled off her torn tunic and black pantaloons and as she felt she must be dirty from the horse-cloth, she washed herself in cold water.

She then put on the nightgown she had been wearing, which was still where she had left it on the floor.

Slipping into bed, she no longer felt limp or afraid,

but excited because the Marquis had said he was coming back.

She waited, thinking how strong and wonderful he was and how, if he had not heard her call for help and come with Chang to save her, she might at this very moment be floating in the stream.

The communicating door opened and he came in.

He was wearing the long red robe he had worn on their wedding-night, and she thought he would come and sit on the bed to talk to her.

Instead he pulled back the curtains from both the windows and she could see stars in the sky and the moonlight that would soon begin to fade.

She thought it would not be much later than three o'clock in the morning, and yet a century seemed to have passed since she had come upstairs to bed.

The Marquis came towards her and now he blew out the candles and before Elmina could say anything he got into bed beside her.

For a moment she was too astonished to move or even be able to think, as his arms went round her and he pulled her against him.

It was then she felt herself quiver because she could feel the hardness of his body against hers.

"Now, my precious," the Marquis said, and his voice was very deep, "we can talk about what has happened, if that is what you want. Actually all I want is to kiss you!"

"Please . . . kiss me," Elmina whispered.

She tipped back her head as she spoke and her lips were ready and waiting for his.

As if there were no hurry, his mouth was very

gentle against the softness of hers.

Yet once again a shaft of lightning seemed to shoot through her, half a rapture and half a pain.

Then Elmina felt his lips become more possessive, more demanding.

She knew this was what she would have never known if she had died, and she felt as if her whole being leapt with a strange ecstasy towards him.

As he kissed her and went on kissing her she surrendered herself completely and absolutely to his magnificence.

Every second his lips became more demanding, more insistent.

Now Elmina could feel not only the lightning shooting through her body, but a warmth rising within her which became a flame burning its way through her breasts, up into her lips so that it met the flame on his.

She knew suddenly that a fire raged within the Marquis also and this was what she had longed for but had thought would never happen.

He paused for a moment to look down at her, and she whispered:

"I... love you... how can I help but... love you?"

"As I cannot help loving you."

She felt herself stiffen against him. Then he said:

"That was what you wanted, was it not, my precious, that I should love you as I have never loved anyone before? And that is exactly what has happened!"

"Is it... true... really true?"

"I think you would know if I were not speaking

the truth," the Marquis replied. "I swear to you by everything in which I believe that what I feel for you is different from anything I have ever felt for any other woman."

Elmina gave a cry of happiness. Then she asked: "Are you sure? Are you . . . really sure?"

"It is what you told me I should feel, and actually it is what I have been feeling for a long time."

"Why . . . did you not . . . tell me?"

"I wanted to be absolutely sure of myself, and also that you would not want to fight against me as you did before."

Elmina gave a little laugh.

"It was Karate which saved my life tonight, and the thoughts which we know are part of that . . . strange science."

"It was Chang who heard you and brought me to you."

"Is that what . . . happened?"

"Chang came to my bedroom and told me you were in danger, and when we reached the stable-yard we found the Arab mare gone and Hogson's small son had seen you being carried away."

"They took me with them because I had seen their faces," Elmina said. "Then because I was slowing the speed at which they wished to travel they . . . decided to . . . kill me."

As if the Marquis could not bear any more, his lips came down on hers.

Now he was kissing her frantically, which she knew came from his fear of what might have happened.

He kissed her until her heart beat so violently that

she felt as if she could no longer keep it within her breast.

He held her closer and closer and she knew there was no further need of words between them.

Because they were so close, it was as if their bodies, their hearts and their minds were all linked indivisibly with each other's and they were no longer two people, but one.

This was love as she had always longed for it, love as she had always believed it could be in all its perfection.

Then as the Marquis carried her up to the stars which seemed to encircle his head she knew that she had found the love that she had always known was different and for which she had searched in her dreams.

* * *

A long time later the stars had faded, the moon had vanished and the pale fingers of the dawn sun were sweeping away the dark of the night.

The sky outside the window was the colour of Elmina's hair.

The Marquis, feeling it soft beneath his hand, said:

"Dawn has broken, my beautiful one, and I think we both know it is the dawn of a new life for both of us."

"Is that why you . . . pulled back the . . . curtains?"

"I want you to feel you belonged first to the stars, then to the sun," he said gently, "and although something ugly and unpleasant has happened to you, it is of no importance and you can forget it."

Elmina gave a cry.

"How could you think of anything so wonderful, so beautiful?" she asked.

"It is how you have taught me to think," the Marquis said, "you and Chang. I realise now I have so much more to learn and there is so much more to know."

Elmina laughed.

"Not from me," she said. "I am your pupil, and you will always, as you well know, be the Master."

"I am very content to teach you about love, my beautiful wife," the Marquis said, "but in all else, like a star in the sky, you must guide and inspire me."

"Can I do . . . that?"

"You have done so already! Ever since I first met you it seems as though we have known each other for years—no, centuries! You have changed my way of thinking, and I know that life for both of us in the future is going to be an adventure, and what undoubtedly you will consider a challenge!"

Elmina drew in her breath.

She knew that this was what she had wanted for the Marquis, this was what would stop him from becoming bored and supercilious.

She drew a little closer to him as she said:

"There is so much I want to . . . learn about love . . . I did not know it could be so . . . wonderful . . . even though I suspected it might be . . . like this."

"Like what?" the Marquis asked.

"Like . . . being high in the sky amongst the stars

". . . or moving towards the sun."

She pressed her cheek against his bare shoulder as she whispered:

"When you . . . excite me I can feel the . . . sunshine burning in my . . . breasts."

"As you make me burn, my lovely one."

The light in the window grew stronger and he turned a little so that he could see her more clearly as he smoothed her long hair away from her forehead.

"How can you be so different," he asked, "not only in the way you look, which enchants me, but also in the way you think and feel?"

"I want to be . . . different for you," Elmina said impulsively.

"You *are* different! I want to write a poem, paint a picture, compose a Concerto to that difference, because there are no words in which I can express exactly what I feel."

"How can you . . . say such things to . . . me?"

"I am saying them because they are true."

Then as he looked at her and saw that her eyes were filled with tears he asked:

"My darling, what have I said to make you cry?"

"They are . . . tears of . . . happiness. All my life no one had ever . . . loved me . . . no one has ever said such . . . perfect . . . wonderful things that I shall . . . never . . . ever forget!"

"I shall say a great many more now that I have started," the Marquis said, "and, let me add, that is something very unusual for me!"

She knew he was trying to laugh at himself and she put out her hands to draw his head down to hers.

"I have loved you ever since I first . . . saw you when I was a . . . little girl," she whispered. "But in all those years when I thought about you and dreamt about you . . . I never realised how . . . marvellous you really were . . . or how . . . fine and . . . noble."

"I am afraid you are flattering me," the Marquis said. "At the same time, my darling, that is what I want to be for you."

"Then . . . please, will you teach me to be everything you desire in your most . . . secret dreams so that I shall never . . . disappoint you?"

"I am quite certain you will never do that. You have surprised, astonished and enchanted me ever since we were married. Now we are starting out on a voyage of discovery, you and I, which begins with our thoughts and ends with our thoughts, and which will take us through this life and a number of others until we reach eternity."

Elmina gave a cry.

"That is the heart of the science of Karate!" she exclaimed. "That is what the monks believed . . . and why I know that wherever our voyage of discovery leads us we shall . . . find what we . . . seek."

"We will find it . . . together."

The Marquis pulled her closer to him, and he spoke as if the things they had said excited him not only mentally but also physically.

He moved his hand gently over her body and he was kissing not only her lips, but her eyes and her cheeks, and then the softness of her neck.

He felt her thrill with new sensations she had not known before, and yet were still part of the wonder and the ecstasy he made her feel every time he touched her.

She moved closer to him, then realised that the Marquis was looking at her as if searching her face and looking into the strangeness of her eyes.

"I adore you, my very unusual wife!" he said softly.

Then as she looked up at him adoringly, his lips were on hers, and she felt again her whole being leap towards him like a flame she could not control.

As the sun rose, they were part of it, and its burning glory swept through them.

Then there was only the love that is Eternal thought and for which there is no end.

ABOUT THE AUTHOR

Barbara Cartland, the world's most famous romantic novelist, who is also an historian, playwright, lecturer, political speaker and television personality, has now written over 370 books and sold over 370 million books the world over.

She has also had many historical works published and has written four autobiographies as well as the biographies of her mother and that of her brother, Ronald Cartland, who was the first Member of Parliament to be killed in the last war. This book has a preface by Sir Winston Churchill and has just been republished with an introduction by Sir Arthur Bryant.

Love at the Helm, a novel written with the help and inspiration of the late Admiral of the Fleet, the Earl Mountbatten of Burma, is being sold for the Mountbatten Memorial Trust.

Miss Cartland in 1978 sang an Album of Love Songs with the Royal Philharmonic Orchestra.

In 1976 by writing twenty-one books, she broke the world record and has continued for the following seven years with twenty-four, twenty, twenty-three, twenty-four, twenty-four, twenty-five, and twenty-three. She is in the *Guinness Book of Records* as the best-selling author in the world.

She is unique in that she was one and two in the Dalton List of Best Sellers, and one week had four books in the top twenty.

In private life Barbara Cartland, who is a Dame of the Order of St. John of Jerusalem, Chairman of the St. John Council in Hertfordshire and Deputy President of the St. John Ambulance Brigade, has also fought for better conditions and salaries for Midwives and Nurses.

Barbara Cartland is deeply interested in Vitamin Therapy and is President of the British National Association for Health. Her book *The Magic of Honey* has sold throughout the world and is translated into many languages. Her designs "Decorating with Love" are being sold all over the U.S.A., and the National Home Fashions League named her in 1981, "Woman of Achievement."

Barbara Cartland's Romances (a book of cartoons) has recently been published in Great Britain and the U.S.A., as well as *Getting Older, Growing Younger*, and a cookery book, *The Romance of Food*.

BARBARA CARTLAND

Called after her own
beloved Camfield Place,
each Camfield novel of love
by Barbara Cartland
is a thrilling, never-before published
love story by the greatest romance
writer of all time.

April '85...THE PERIL AND THE PRINCE
May '85...ALONE AND AFRAID
June '85...TEMPTATION OF A TEACHER

More romance from
BARBARA CARTLAND